THE GIFT
OF
WOMEN

THE GIFT
OF
WOMEN

GEORGE McWHIRTER

EXILE
editions
Fiction, Poetry, Translation, Drama and Nonfiction

Library and Archives Canada Cataloguing in Publication

McWhirter, George, author
The gift of women / George McWhirter.

Short stories.
Issued in print and electronic formats.
ISBN 978-1-55096-425-7 (pbk.).--ISBN 978-1-55096-428-8 (pdf).--
ISBN 978-1-55096-426-4 (epub).--ISBN 978-1-55096-427-1 (mobi)

I. Title.

PS8575.W48G53 2014   C813'.54   C2014-904192-6
C2014-904193-4

Design and composition by Mishi Uroboros
Cover art by Olena Vizerskaya
Typeset in Minion and Perpetua Titling fonts at Moons of Jupiter Studios

Published by Exile Editions Ltd ~ www.ExileEditions.com
144483 Southgate Road 14–GD, Holstein, Ontario, N0G 2A0
Printed and Bound in Canada in 2014, by Imprimerie Gauvin

We gratefully acknowledge, for their support toward our publishing activities,
the Canada Council for the Arts, the Government of Canada through
the Canada Book Fund (CBF), the Ontario Arts Council,
and the Ontario Media Development Corporation.

Canadian Sales: The Canadian Manda Group, 165 Dufferin Street,
Toronto ON M6K 3H6 www.mandagroup.com 416 516 0911

North American and International Distribution, and U.S. Sales:
Independent Publishers Group, 814 North Franklin Street,
Chicago IL 60610 www.ipgbook.com toll free: 1 800 888 4741

TO ANGELA AND HER FRIENDS

ARRIVEDERCI

Re: *Deilf* as observed St. Colum Cille in a stream swollen by rains in the vicinity of Bangor and its recently established abbey, subsequently recorded in this elaboration.

River dolphin return to their small streams when they rise in great rains. Sometime these returns take decades or centuries, to come, but as we know, though it never changes, the dolphin appearance is always in keeping with those times in which they reappear.

—From the Irish. Anonymous, Iona, AD 599

Meta had four or five misdemeanours against her. Dalliance with U.S. soldiers was growled about, daily, but unpunishable – unless Meta could be got up for running a bawdy bungalow. When they discovered she had sloped in with a foreigner, not by way of her front door, but the river around the back, they thought they had her for espionage and harbouring an alien.

Still, they didn't actually see her smuggle him in or hold out her hand to help him up the stone steps she had put in to kneel on and do her washing in the river. They'd have taken the fella for a visiting dignitary, a dark prince, arriving by water to take her to the Town Ball in Bangor or the Plaza in Belfast, where girls danced their legs off with anything in bellbottoms, air force blue or khaki.

Dressed in his blue-black sweater, thick worsted trousers and wool toque, they might also have spotted him as one of those Italian frogmen, who had dumped his wet-suit and goggles somewhere so that he might land and blend in. The toque, which he never took off, appeared to cover a bald head or hair so close cropped it shone as bluely as the wool toque on top. The sideburns, razored so each jutted down his jaws like a jackboot, had cinched his nationality for Meta.

He was an *I-tie*.

Meta's was a mecca for anything beginning with *"i"*: anything *in*solent, *ill*egal, *ir*regular or *in*decent. How illegal, improper or improvident was chalked up on lavatory walls, milestones, under railway arches and the slate in Redman's shop, where Meta owed a small fortune.

"She'd slide into bed with any pair of odd balls – it's second nature to her," said Mrs. McLarnen as Mrs. Redmond cut and paddled a square of butter for her, then stamped her ration book.

"More's the pity she isn't in it for the money. It'd wipe her slate clean with me."

So, their getting wind of the crime after the fact, when the *enemy alien* had done a bunk, made the story one more

Meta myth the village of Carnalea chalked up to her second nature.

At Whin Hill Meta stands to shower her head. The stream divides in two around it before joining again to flow over a tiny delta of stones to the sea. The wind beats her skirt against her thighs. A storm has been and gone in the night, and on the morning tide the American aircraft carrier weighed anchor and went with it. Meta is watching the carrier clear the horizon. The sky goes bluer and the sea, too – not summer blue, but cold-as-a-mackerel winter blue, whose contagious colour everything on land and water catches, everything, except the yellow whin. This is why she doesn't see y'r man, dressed in navy blues. He gleams, either because he is soaking wet, or his woollens are saturated in lanolin or woven from short fine hairs sleek as seal skin. One moment, the only sound is shallow water running across the stones below, then their tops clack and grate as his feet slither over them in a pair of deep blue swimming pool slippers.

Cox, the retired Major in the big-windowed house above, uses them to walk down his path and wade in here. The Major also uses his binoculars to watch the coast for things washing in. Will he see this bit of jetsam who's waded ashore under his own steam? Vapour rises from his mouth and slowly off the toque at the top of his head. Where's he from – the carrier? An American deserter? Or one of those poor souls from the submarines, deserting Italy now that it's losing, like slaves off a sinking galley?

Meta calls to him, but the gurgled answer could be the river's or something like Italian. She picks her way down, takes off her shoes to stand beside him in her bare feet. He looks down at them on the cold stone. "Feet," "sweet," "cheep?" She can't catch it, but will have to take him up to her house by the river, to hear what he has to say and see what she can do. "Italian," she asks, "*Ital-iano*?" She has him under the arm. "Were you after the American carrier?"

"*Deilf*," he says. She wrinkles her nose. He wrinkles his nose back at her and touches the top of his toque to scratch the wool there. "Brass Eel," he says next, and studies her face to see if this registers.

"Pull the other leg, Basil," she tells him, but he shivers and she feels sorry for him. She puts her hand on his toque. "Did you fall off? Get left behind?" she asks when his eyes roll up to where her hand is laid on his toque. "You were after the American carrier. I was after the carrier myself. Ended up, same as you, just watching it bugger off."

She points up the river. When she stops pulling him by the arm and pushes ahead of him, he matches her step. The thin, shaggy shanks of the hawthorns intrigue him as much as her heels. He stares up and touches the crimson haws.

"It must be dark in the water. Specially at night?" says Meta. "Bet you're glad you're here in Carnalea."

"Carn-allee."

"Not Carn-allee, Car-na-lea." She looks into his eyes. "Are you a singer?" They approach the tunnel that goes under the railway line. "A tenor, a Benjamino Gigli? Lovely 'n' all as your voice is, no arias in here. We don't want a living soul to know you're here." She puts her finger to her lips, then points the same finger at the tunnel. The trickle and ripple in the tunnel must amuse him, he chirps and chatters along with it.

At the tunnel's other end, he stops before the opening to the light. Plants that have overgrown the railway station railing dangle into it. Honeysuckle and fuchsia that remind Meta of female private parts and sea things: anemone. He stops her under them with the grip of his hand. She feels the fingers, fine, hard as knitting needles. "Never fear. My bungalow's a couple of houses up. Other side of this tunnel. I'll have you in, out of sight."

Why should she want him in? If he has no ration book, emergency grubstake – she will have to share hers. No tinkle of change in his pocket either. Perhaps the money's sewn into the lining of his trousers, all in notes. "You made off with some treasure? Off those boats the Nazis use to transport loot from everywhere they invaded?"

Meta sighs. She would steal all she could, off them nasties – every brass tack. She hopes his pockets have little velvet pouches tied up with string. She's seen pirates in the pictures empty them onto tavern tables. "Diamonds?" she asks.

"Dye-a-monds," he replies and Meta beams. He undulates in a Carmen Miranda samba. And as they say in the movies, she can't keep her eyes off his rhythm section. "You know Harry James, Betty Grable?" But before he can answer, she says, "Both of us better samba inside."

He looks at the whitewashed stones bordering the back garden path. They wiggle toward the river and the steps she uses to do her washing. The neighbours will be watching the front for her, as usual. They peer over their hedges to see her head pass by with the different types of military headgear. They guess what service, what rank by the cap beside Meta's turban. Out of pride, Meta never brings anyone in by the back door, but Basil is special. On her back doorstep, he pauses to put his nose high into the air.

Sniffing the state of her bungalow, is he?

"Any Ardglass herrin'!" comes the Wednesday call from the fish cart. The neighbour women won't have seen a thing. They're on the road, or at their gates, plates ready for the herring. No dirty newspaper parcels for them, straight to the plate and into the pan.

Meta watches Basil twitch his nose and ears. Maybe he thinks the Ardglass herrin'-howl is a siren. The fishmonger's son prolongs it, like he's offering the Carnalea women the love of their lives. "Anyyyyyaaaaah Aaaardglaaaaas heeeeru-uuuuun?" He makes one stop for each stretch of road between the bends in it. He collects the women's plates, like a clergyman his alms takers' at the altar on a Sunday. Meta always elbows and upsets the others' plates so badly, they give her leeway.

"It's only the herrin' man."

This information catches Basil twisting from side to side.

"Kar-na-lee, dye-a-mond, ear-ring man," he says.

"Not an ear-ring man, it's th' Ardglass 'errin' man. I didn't forget it's Wednesday. I have the money to get some." She nods at the back door. "I'll get a plate and buy a dozen – a dozen and a half. That'll do us a day or two."

The herring only last one meal and the last is gone before the first has hit the pan.

"You're that starvin', you ate them raw? Sweet Jesus – an extra mouth to feed that swallows herring like I do Aspirin!"

Meta's ambition for the title, "Kept Woman," is gone. She has ended up with a hungry man on her hands again.

"Is Basil your real name?" she asks him after their meal together on that Wednesday.

"*Deilf*," he tells her.

"That's only initials for something, your second name. Is Basil the first, the Christian name?"

"Boto," says he.

"Boat – Oh! " she says back to him. He nods and still hasn't taken off his toque, nor sweater for that matter.

"*Deilf*, del-feen…"

"Del. Lots of yanks are called Del. I'm not sure what it's short for. Delanore, like Roosevelt? Feen, now… Feeney? Did you run away there from Mussolini, like our ice-cream men, the Capronis, in Bangor?" She claps her hand over his mouth when he begins to flute and whistle. She puts her mouth where her hand was and Basil Del Feeney swings her and dances with her on his mouth. He sets her on her feet, sways her, then has her rolling to his muted whistles and flutes in one ear after the other. Side to side, on her back, on her belly, rocking like a boat to move it forward with nary a sail nor an oar, just a barge pole, Meta laughs. The energy he puts into her!

What do the old biddies say over the tops of their hedges to her buying the last box of herring off the fishmonger on his way back up the road – "Feeding the fleet with those, are ye, Meta?"

When she wakes at 0300 hours, she sees he is gone. Air force men are forever taking off at 0300 to get to Limavady before it's 0600. As far as they're concerned, Northern Ireland is just one big aircraft carrier. When she gets up, goes out, walks up her front steps and is standing on the road, there are no plates, no herring cart – Wednesday is gone like a very fishy dream and what did she do with the box of herring she spent her rainy day dough on?

She sticks out her tongue at the emptiness of Station Road.

Back down the concrete steps she goes to the house, through the house to the back door, opens it and Basil steps in.

"So, you're 'stablishin' a base of operations, are you?"

Before she gets any louder, he puts his mouth on hers to stop her. Meta feels terrible, lying beside him naked, a moment after that. He gleams with something, too – sweat, or grease. What you'd expect from the I-ties and their olive oil. Should she go on about her aiding and abetting, give him a towel, or a pot scrub?

Basil Del Feeney does have the blue jaw of a Mussolini and the regular run of bad men in the pictures. Has Basil-me-boy planted limpet mines, reconnoitered and reported on the building of the latest carrier on the slips at Harland & Wolff's shipyard?

The hull for those hulks gets launched first and the rest, put together on the water like an iron aerodrome. Like a city – with more people in them than Bangor. Which reminds her! She'll need to go see the Ardglass herring man, but in his Bangor shop.

Except… Meta's back door smells like a fishmonger's already, and pushing the door wide to take a geek, she shoves it into a pack of dead mackerel, lying with the gubs wide open on her teeny back porch. She swears, come the next night, she'll stay awake, but in due course, after he comes and comes, her eyelids buckle, she blinks, wakes and the night and himself are gone again.

Time for a nip of the moonshine, the night life in the morning.

She has this bottle of poteen the policeman, Hagen, left her – that time he had her up in court for keeping a dog without a licence. Poor Rex, who ran away from her in the end and got run over, but brought policeman Hagen with the news and the poteen to sympathize.

She needed a pet, Hagen said. Tucked in together, sipping poteen, the sergeant declared, "I'm your pet policeman." Now, it's Basil Del Feeney, who shows up next morning with a mother-of-pearl shell big as a dinner plate. Two lobsters snap and squirm on it: green, beady-eyed – colour of ocean jade, clicking like typists or flamenco dancers.

Meta is not without skill or education. She has shorthand, went to Pitman's, but without fail, in her secretarial career, some dirty git of a manager would want her to use her longhand on him and promise her all sorts of things for the job. As she slow boils the lobsters to a coma and empties the shell of meat, he watches her closely. What's he puzzled about? The knack Meta has in her fingers that he can put to use setting timers, attaching wires to detonators? Suddenly, the red lobsters gape like gutted cities at Meta, like Belfast in the Blitz, shattered – these blazing red shells. And feeling instantly guilty, she throws the shells and plundered contents in his face, which just as instantly makes her sorry for his burning hunger for seafood and fucking.

As bad as beating Rex, the dog, with its ham bone for dinner.

But Basil believes Meta's celebrating and tosses the shredded meat over her head like shellfish confetti. From feeling dubious, to devastated, to damn well delighted, Meta decides this is as mad as a marriage for her, at last.

Basil's mating rhythm with her works in sets of seven, regular as waves, and the fizz in her blood is as strong as when her bare skin met the Atlantic on a summer jaunt to the beach at Buncrana. Like dunking her bum in champagne –

such sizzle between her skin and the sea, she stayed flushed for hours afterwards, singing all the way back through Counties Derry and Antrim to Down. And as Major Cox of the big-windowed house on the shore put it: "set her effervescent ass on the lap of all and sundry in the charabanc."

In bed after dinner, she picks slivers of shell from Basil's toque. If she lifts the toque a smidgen, his eyes open and he coos like a sea pigeon. Otherwise he sleeps soundly, but always with the toque on. Like the cloth cap working men wear at all hours – to sleep and to work in. Meta might have expected different, but loves Basil Del Feeney none the less. Still, she needs something more to show for it. A girl can only stare so long at mother-of-pearl, mackerel, sole and giant frigging halibut he hauls to her back door. She pours verdigris over the back step to kill the stink.

But still no proposal, no statement of intent!

Then, would she understand one if he gave it to her, verbally or written in his titillating jibber of Italian or whatever it is? Since none seems to be in the offing, Meta will make a bond of blood, a blood bond as she rummages in a kitchen drawer for the filleting knife she'll sharpen with spit on a cake of carborundum. He won't feel a thing.

In the bedroom, it is 0100 hours.

He's at it again, after the old bum and belly samba, whistling off like a tugboat, chugging into that little sleep that seduces her into the same. Tonight, however, Meta cuts a stroke on his bare upper arm, then one on hers. At the same time, she lies down beside him to make a seal with their blood, shoulder to shoulder, like Siamese twins.

And what does Basil Del Feeney do?

He wakens. He sees the dried blood. He chirps, he chitters and he weeps.

"Jesus, the Axis Powers sent a cry-baby like you to frogman for them!"

But she can tell he thinks it's her marking him as hers. And, how would she feel if some lover notched her up to his conquests in her sleep? But that's not the way of it. She's cutting him into her life long-time, not short-time – blood bonding them together. Look, she's cut her arm the same, close to the shoulder, and pressed it to his, Siamese twinning a tiny wee bit of what flows from both their hearts and minds inside them, but that's not how he takes it.

He looks at his shoulder and at hers, like she's not cut him in, but cut him out, off from something he's staring wide-eyed at in the dark – his eyes like two big jellyfish. The noise of him gives her a head-buster of a headache. It's no human sound. Never mind the Hoeys and the Carscaddens next door hearing it – out at sea, they'll pick it up on that newfangled detector for submarine noise. And Meta's slap dab in the middle of the bed with it.

She has to get up and get herself a headache powder.

On the cutting board in the kitchen, she chops the twist off the blue packet with the carving knife. Tips it straight into her mouth, instead of pouring it into a cup. She tips three more powders till they are all done and goes through the same routine at the Redmond's counter the next morning – three in a row, and she needs more.

She stands back, away from the counter at Redmond's shop, waiting for them, and is scrolled up and down by the eyes of all who come in and out for their messages. She puts up with the chinging of the doorbell to give Basil the option of an exit while she's at Redmond's away from his piercing cheep and chitter.

They've all heard it, but don't say.

The shoppers believe Meta is raising budgies, which doesn't make sense to them. Budgies that eat herring is the only evidence they have. There are those that raise budgies by the hundred, for sale. They imagine Meta's bungalow, hiving with yellow budgies and white budgie shit. Like everything else, Meta's brought it on herself.

"It's the budgies," they say, "isn't it, Meta? Them budgies are the bugger. Wouldn't you be better keeping hens and selling the eggs?" they ask her out of nowhere, expecting Meta to answer as she stands with her back to the sliding panel for the display window

"Where would I put the bloody run – in the river?" Meta tells them, then moans, "That's the only run room I have."

She makes sense to them, for once. They shut up and watch her face to keep up with the progress of her headache after she has downed the powders.

A budgie head-buster.

God knows who brought her this chirpy wee gift, but Meta's sunken eyes are as guarded as a cave with moonraker's treasure. The longer Meta stands, the more she disturbs Mrs. Redmond. But Mrs. Redmond lets her be because Meta might disclose something worth waiting to hear.

The poor women who get into the breeding business.

They've read about them in the newspapers they buy at Redmond's. That ladies' tailor with the chinchillas she reared for fur coats. The chillas had no proper coop, or whatever they use, so she kept them in her house. They ate her wallpaper, her furniture, nibbled her whole house down around her, then ran away from the home they'd destroyed. If they hadn't sent her to Purdysburn, nothing would be funnier than the ladies' tailor who wanted to be a high-class furrier with her own home-reared fur. Women with their gumption pointed in the wrong direction are shoo-ins for the asylum.

"Are you sure it's budgies and not some bruiser?" one customer asks over her shoulder, as she pulls open the door and rings its brass bell going out.

They look at Meta.

"Or a squealer?" the next one asks as her parting shot.

But what kind of squealer – a traitor, an IRA informer for the Jerries?

More likely the regular kind of squealer they all had. The squealer for his dinner, squealer for his tea, squealer for his friggin' fags from the shop.

"Here, have one on me." Mrs. Redmond's daughter hands Meta another blue twist with a headache powder in it.

He's there when she gets back, staring at his arm, holding the streak of crusted blood to his nose. He snorts at it, but the noise comes out of his toque.

"Basil Del Feeney, you're still stark naked and it's one o'clock."

He turns his look toward his sweater, trousers, glossy, patent rubber slippers as if they're to blame for abandoning his body. "I'm going to put some vinegar in a pot," she says, then goes into the kitchen and puts some vinegar in a pot, sets it on a hob of the gas stove. The kitchen is no bigger than a galley on a little boat. Its pungency will help her head and she'll put one cloth soaked in it on his arm and the other on her forehead. Our Lord gave vinegar the power to do for others what it couldn't do for him – take away the pain.

"Vinegar is a miracle," she tells Basil Del Feeney.

"Vine-gar mir-acle,"

"You know I didn't mean to. I got greedy for your rhythm section," she says. "I had no right to want it permanent on my tum-tum," she says to him in her talking-to-children's voice.

"No right," he repeats, and sounds too much like a budgie for her liking. A blue parrot she has picked up out of the sea.

All this recuperation from a little nick. Feeding him fish-soup over and over nauseates her. A cat, at least, can take a turn at bread dipped in a saucer of milky tea. But the bones, the eyes, and the livers. He has to have them. In no days' time she's convinced again it was a bad idea to have a man in her bungalow.

"Once in the door," her Ma told her, "they're tyrannical invalids." No, her Ma went one better: "*Titanic* invalids!"

"The debilitation of love," the minister in the Carnalea Methodist Church said one time in his sermon, while Meta was still a going member of the congregation. "Jesus suffered from the incurable weakness of love for man."

Meta snickered at that and got elbowed by her mother.

Basil Del Feeney is after something. He wants out of bed. He wants to show her what it is he wants. He draws it for her with his finger. He draws squares in the air in front of her face. A sheet of squared paper is what he wants, a paper they can play X's and O's on.

He splays the fingers of one hand and crosses them with the other, he swings his fingers like a cat's cradle. A sheet of paper that swings? No. A net is what he wants, a net that swings! What's a net that swings – a hammock – what every lazy-arsed Latin lover likes to lie and do fuck all in, once they have some bitch to do the work for them!

"You want a bloody hammock?"

But she can't be angry at him. He's wasting away. Hardly a day gone by and he's wasting in spite of two doses of fish soup, whelks, mussels, dulse – clams, rock cod, eels from under the stones for snacks. She's got to go back into Bangor and back to work at old Furey's pub. She's been a week away already. Old Furey wants her back behind the bar, her bosom there to bump up the take. She can't be sneaking by old Furey's to Sharkey, the Ship's Chandler's, next door!

But she could go to a chandler's in Belfast.

"Do you want brass rings to go with it?" she asks Basil Del Feeney.

"So, have you taken on an extra hand who needs a hammock?" the chandler's helper asks while Meta examines the brass blowers and compasses with her finger. The way she has her breasts thrust up with her corset, Meta could pose as a siren or ship's figurehead for sale, but she only aims to lead the chandler's man on – to see if it leads to a discount.

"If I have, will I get trade rate?"

"I won't say I can't say yes," he tells her very slowly, then asks, "Your vessel is called?"

"HMS *Del Feeney*."

"And your new hand's name is?"

"Basil Del Feeney."

"And what does the boat trade in – dopey monikers or silly monkeys?"

They both laugh.

"Perhaps I can assist you mounting the item after you purchase it?"

"You'll have to get the train and come to Carnalea with me to do that."

"Perhaps a demonstration here will do instead. I'll give you trade rate, if you'll just come in the back and pick your hammock."

He says his perhapses as though they are made of truly juicy pears and happy hapses.

The midnight shadow on Del Feeney's chin is dry, bristly and blotched. Sickening smudges mottle his back and shoulders. He has her hang the hammock over the back stoop, but looks no happier in it, just darker because of the gloomy outdoors and the rain.

He still chitters. He's not cold, hasn't got a cold. He's just shrivelling and Meta has begun to connect his chitters to the rain, which has been on since she nicked him and left for Belfast. The river has risen over the edge of her garden, stirring around her whitewashed stones on the river bank, drowning and deadening their colour.

By the morning, her garden is thoroughly flooded and Del Feeney's gone.

In his place – a peace offering, an ugly great tuna fish swinging in the hammock, like Basil caught it flying through the air in the dark. For God's sake, it's nothing so edible as a tuna, it's a damn dolphin not even a magician could cut into nice frying steaks. After her going to the trouble of installing a hammock, he only wanted it to go fishing for his farewell. The dolphin has a fin on it like a plough share, and Basil's frigging toque like a blue bye-bye note stuck over its blowhole, suffocating the poor beast. Its nose is poking through a hole in the mesh.

Does Meta find the thing ugly because she's lumped with it as this heart-wrenching, likely back-breaking, very ugly gift? Your dolphin's not like your nice tuna. They have fins like little ballet dancer's feet. They do *pas de dousies* in the sea on them.

She flips the hammock and is immediately sorry. The slap makes the back porch's floor boards jump loose from their nails. The river gives a swollen aargh. "Aargh," Meta gargles back at it as she heaves the dolphin's tail and body behind it down the back porch steps until she stands shin deep in water, in her own sopping garden.

The wet makes the grass as slippery as sea weed. She feels mud between her toes; the grass she hasn't cut all summer winds around her ankles. So what if the damn dolphin doesn't like it, the slime makes it easier for her, but it's beyond comprehension what a man will lumber a woman with.

Now, the dolphin flails. The slide and roll of the swollen river sends the stones all over her grass in a jumbled underwater game of bowls. One hits her shin. She curses the muddied whitewash on it.

At last, she has the animal in the stream. It beats against it, in the wrong direction. Never do a dumb bloody dolphin a good turn. Where's the intelligence, the sixth sense they're supposed to have. But it's sick, brains all dried out from being fished out and trussed up all night in a hammock. Once it spouts and spits, and unclogs the old blowhole of the toque, it'll see its way clear. The old toque whirled around it like caught there in a whirlpool

"What did he stick that frigging toque there with?"

Spit hits her in the face "You're welcome," Meta says to it. "And if you see that rotten bastard, tell him I hope he blows himself up."

Away the dolphin goes, taking flood and rain behind it, whistling something close to arrivederci, over and over, through the tunnel under the Belfast County Down Railway, between the red-berried hawthorns and past Whin Hill. But that could also be the 9 o'clock train tooting as it passes over the top and the passengers gaze out at the awfully odd level of the water down below.

Sittings for
A PHOTOGRAPH
IN A GREEN ROOM

Ms. Tina Martin,
44 Hambly Close,
London WC 4.

September 16, 1977

Dear Tina,

How is John? William is well, the children have gone back to school and I have time to turn this over in my mind. Do you ever stare out of the window until the children come home, but never think about them once? If this carries on, even though I'm thousands of miles away in British Columbia, I'll end up with Sally, a stone's throw from Belfast in Downpatrick, mired in madness and troubles – not *The Troubles*: the Wellesley sisters', Geraldine and Sally's oldest, and latest.

I've always only been able to talk to you about her, Tina. In school, and in snippets over I don't know how many letters and tapes, like I do now. You understood when Sally was a teen and turning into what she is. Talking to Mummy was like addressing a bottle of perfume, something rigid and reeking and totally glazed. Daddy was better, but Sally did to him what Mummy must have done ages ago, bamboozled and paralysed him with guilt at his own weakness.

When winters came, Daddy used to say she was like one of the summer chairs left out in the rain: the paint shone brighter than in the sunshine. It sort of shocks to see it. Do you let the poor thing be, or take it in? Once you put it away, the empty spot stares at you. That's how I feel about what I've just done to my sister.

Mrs. Moir, the neighbour, phoned to tell us she hadn't seen either of them in weeks. We knew that these past few years Sally left Daddy to wander the rest of the house while she moved into the Green Room. That's where Mrs. Moir and the constable found her naked and soaked in Johnson's Baby Oil.

You know the story behind that.

I'll stop typing this. I have to make a set of phone calls for the Vancouver, Point Grey Little League. Children's baseball, not dwarfs, Tina. Even though it is British Columbia, we play American games over here.

NEXT DAY, SEPTEMBER 17

Sorry, Tina. I had to do some driving on top of the phoning.

You know the Green Room. The room, where Mother kept the photograph of her in the nude as a challenge to every woman who stepped into it, Sally and I, especially. Would we ever have anything to match it? Or were we expected to add our nakedness – the two missing muses', and twirl in a same delirium of vanity from the maypole of our youth?

The shot was taken in 1934 when Mother was 19. We saw it when we were the same age, but did either you or I feel it daring us to strip, fold our legs under us on the floor, and pull our hair up over our head to hold it high and tight in our fists?

Sister Sally did.

Daddy said the whole tasteless tableau was to show the woman in the frame was fit to be hung, or have her head chopped off for being such a biddy and posing in the nude.

Well, Sally certainly lost hers.

I hated the Green Room. Even if I had to sit with Daddy snoring in the living room when I was home. You know how I played pairs and singles, tennis and shuttlecock, summer and winter with you. It was so I could come home and collapse with you at your house, it was why I became a champion, mad keen on tournaments – to keep me out of our house. And I never got on a train because I didn't want to meet Mummy on the platform, or in a carriage, coming down from Belfast. She would meet Daddy for dinner after he closed his book for the day at Wellesley Ads. Then, she stayed on at the Grand Hotel or the Abercorn like she was one of his promotions. He left, worn-out, to go home alone in the car and let her go on drinking.

He spent years socializing just to keep an eye on her. A pity for my poor sister that Daddy was too old and exhausted with no will left to watch over Sally for life.

They were already in their forties when we came along. Mummy had us – just as if a last call for orders had been shouted. Always the last minute, that was Mummy's style. Same as her arriving home on the last train – the Station Master took her arm to the gate and locked it when she went through. She had us late because she didn't want to lose her "lines." She talked about them as if they were out of some poem and not to do with her face or shape.

They were still there though.

Sometimes young men would be too drunk to see the details. They noticed the red hair and the silhouette, and they escorted her onto the train, hoping for God knows what from this middle-aged lady in a sheath dress with enough floral pattern on it to do a botanical garden!

There was this awful skinny one, in a B Special uniform, with his revolver dragging him to the ground. He armed-guarded her right down to the house. They teetered along like twins. He was tall and emaciated, dripping with fingers and elegant gestures, for all his guns and holster. Daddy saw something in this Thomas Tallboy Slattery, or so he wrote. He included a cartoon like the ones he used to draw for *The Belfast Telegraph* before Wellesley Advertising swallowed all his talent for the picture and the punch line. His Slattery cartoon went: IRISHMAN IN UNIFORM, USING POLICE AS A RUNG ON THE SOCIAL LADDER, CLIMBING SHAKILY WITH A

FIREARM IN HAND. Daddy always wrote the best captions, and I quote. On the strength of that impression, Daddy even got down the Oliver Cromwell tankard and let the boyo drink from it.

But when this rakey escort of Mummy's saw Sally, he put his hands up in the air and said, "An athlete. An Amazon!"

And Sally, you know Sally was about as athletic as a crocodile. She just lolled in the sun till she appeared the powerful and the healthy one. That's the shame of it. Sally wanted the looks without the work. She did have a good body. Though not like Mummy's. More comfortable than muscular.

She liked to loll about on the rocks that lay farthest out at the Helen's Bay Beach. On the windiest days, to make her hair blow. It made her look like she was all action without her having to shift herself.

She was famous for that, wasn't she, Tina. And that lamb of hers, Sally's innocence and pastoral purity, paraded about on a string – the poor animal! You couldn't forget it. If she didn't have Mummy's lines and social graces, Sally was wily. People nattered to the lamb and she posed this way and that without saying a sensible word.

And what was it you called her, Tina? Little Go Peep!

When boys followed the wee beast home with her, she took them into the Green Room, where they had to sit blinking at Mummy's belly button in the photo, then at the lamb, then at Sally, then back again.

Sally had a little lamb
But her Mammy had an ass
Its skin was white as snow
And everywhere the Mammy went
Her ass was sure to go.

What would become of anybody, if they had that dirty little ditty trotting behind them on a string?

When it grew into a sheep and too big for the back garden, Daddy had it butchered and the mutton sent to the Sally Ann.

Tina, the timer on the oven has just gone. – Now, where did I get to? Lord, I think I'm doing to you what Daddy did to me every week when he wrote. Except it's all fitted into this one skittery letter.

Sally brought it on herself. There was no way anybody could help her.

She was forever arriving late for school. You saw the shape of that. Year round. No sense of time or place. You know how they called me down to the Office to ask after her whereabouts. I was as clueless as they were, but I couldn't cane her to make her stop – could I? What else could I tell them?

Daddy wrote to stop them pestering me about her.

There was that terrible time when she rented a rowing boat and oared out in front of the school to watch us through binoculars. Like we were dotty little birds behind the Collegiate windows. Mrs. Clegg was declining *pouvoir*: *je peut, tu peut* (put, put, putter, put...) "Isn't that Sally Wellesley out on the water. I recognize her hair."

The wind was blowing it behind her like a flag. I loved school and everybody in our form, Tina. It was in a brilliant location for a school, wasn't it? Top of the hill, overlooking Pickie Pool and Bangor Harbour, but Sally used its pool deck like a runway, and the horseshoe harbour, as Mrs. Clegg put it, like a proscenium stage for her shameless shenanigans. Thank God, the tennis courts were over the hill, away from the water. I know you were a member of the Bangor yacht club and liked watching from the windows of our form room to see which yachts had put out, but you didn't have a sister like Sally.

I'm just too tired, Tina. I'm writing this too late in the evening and I'll have to come back to it tomorrow.

SATURDAY 18

Here I am another day later. Sorry. Do you remember when the boys from the Grammar climbed up the drainpipe into our school attic, then couldn't open the attic door from the inside to get down the stairs and into the school? After they made the mistake of trying to knock it open, the police were called. The Grammar boys were trapped. When the boys tried the drainpipe back down, all the girls were out, looking up it, and the dopes had to be let out by the peelers.

That was like Sally with her captives in the Green Room. She teased boys up to the heights and they couldn't really get down and into the lesson in loveliness she laid on.

They were given a look at nude Mummy in the photo, then Sally sitting in naked competition without her letting them lay a hand on her. After that, a tour of the house, a squint at the Cromwell tankard, and then, they were shown out. Meanwhile, Sally told the lamb fibs about the bad wee boys who had pulled off all her wool.

You know she once told me if Mummy hadn't done anything with men, she would still look like she was in the photograph. If she had stayed innocent as a lamb.

Poor deranged Sally. Do you think pure admiration can keep a woman young?

Sorry I have to break so soon, William is on the phone.

1:30 SAME DAY, BELIEVE IT OR NOT

You remember that Air Corps cadet who got her into the rowing boat so he could wave-hop past her. Ditched her in the water, didn't he, because he skimmed too close. Tina, you went out with the same Queen's Air Corps cadet, before that. He came to pick you up in his uniform, thinking the more dressed up he was the more naked he could get you. Sally showed him more skin and for that he didn't have to wear a thing. Though he got nowhere once he was out of uniform and in the buff beside her, he just clicked into the other half of an arty impression in Sally's head: a *dotty déjeuner sur l'herbe* in the Green Room. After that, when he found out my William's family owned a Cessna, he almost proposed marriage to William and forgot about Sally altogether. I keep expecting to see the fellow here in B.C. where small planes are a way of life. I suppose I flew off and saw less of Sally too once I met William.

You are lucky, though, that you got engaged and married in London. When William came to pick me up, Sally was always trying to lure and Lorelei him, giving him little glances, wearing things that were cut lower and lower till you could practically see her navel. Poor William, who had to stand in the hall, waiting. Remember how he told us, "That girl has a hole in her twice as deep as her cleavage," at the Queen's formal, when she swept by in the arms of one of the Bangor Grammar bunch of engineers.

Not long after the cleavage comment he said she had ambitions to cap her career in the madhouse.

He was cold to everything she said, after she shut him into the Green Room. The one time he walked in to look at Mummy's photo she was standing behind the door and she shut it on him. He came out as silent and white as Mummy's face with her makeup on.

His family had bought interests in big B.C. timber, even then. I suppose they came to the wood, instead of it coming to them. You met William's family, many a time – import Lumber people – down on Queen's Island. We could see their sheds from the train, just after it left the Belfast Co. Down Railway station. You'd titter and say, "I'm glad your William's in wood, but not wooden."

That's about as much as we knew at the time. Later, I learned the family used to trade through Liverpool. The plane, the famous Cessna that fascinated the air cadet, saved time when they checked up on cargoes there. It was easier to buy out of Liverpool. There wasn't the volume in Belfast until the Troubles and the burnings, and every kind of building material grew in demand.

It's odd how Liverpool has died and business at home is kept alive by the bombs that should destroy it.

I still say "home." God, it's an upside-down, hourglass kind of thing being an immigrant. One minute to the next you're not sure what way you see it.

William is busy all the time. I wish I were. You warned me about Training College, about gym teachers being like horses. Once they go lame, their career is shot. Who told you that? It's very good.

I have always been scared to death of being sedentary, or being watched. I'd rather be destroyed. Not Sally. She just wanted to be seen doing nothing at all, with nothing on, like Mummy in the photograph. We should have known where it would go from the rowing boat business. It became a regular thing for her to go out in one, on her own. Remember that time she stood up and took her clothes off in that thunderstorm? Rowed out into the middle of the bay and took off her school uniform.

Naked in the sight of God, I suppose it was. But when I asked her, she told me it was because she was bored. Bored of what? She didn't do anything to be bored of. She played tennis as if she were batting butterflies, no concentration, no focus, and no fun for me. But Sally just smiled secretively, like she had been batting back compliments from the angels. Any roads, Mummy never did that. She always concentrated on some man. She didn't wait around letting the admiration get the better of the action.

What am I saying? What am I writing here? Geraldine Wellesley's objections to her sister going bonkers?

Sorry, Tina. I have to stop now and see who that is at the door.

4:00 P.M.

Any road, Daddy said Sally just slathered herself in baby oil to keep within sniffing distance of the crib.

According to Sally, it was to keep her from burning when she sunbathed. But she put it on to let her shine in the mirror. I know. I'll tell you how she got the idea, from that boy, the weightlifter, who took her to one of those body-building shows. Mr. County Down, or Mr. South Antrim, or something. He let her see how the oil gives muscles extra lines of definition. He's the weightlifter one I wrote to you about after you had taken the chief jewellery buyer's job at Selfridges, the one who wanted my calves because his own legs were too thin and didn't respond to calf presses. I told him to take up tennis or play football in the mud. But what he said – "respond to calf presses" – made me see poor calves in these presses being squished. Even though I know these exercise routines very well from Jordanstown, and Mrs. Brand's lectures on "musculature." It made me giggle at him. He was none too happy. William called him the Greek god on the dog-bone legs.

Now I remember, he met her years before at Crawfordsburn Beach. He was the same bodybuilder who used to drive her up from there to Belfast, through Holywood on his motorbike, no hands, while he used them to comb his hair. I asked Sally why she didn't borrow the comb.

Did you ever believe there were so many narcissi in Northern Ireland? As Miss Arthur, our history teacher, would say – "It is on the bare rocks that we find the brighter lichens growing."

It's true, you forget how vain they are at home. The Ulster lot polish their flaws like they are the facets of diamonds – and they're such a cutting, cruel lot to each other. That's Daddy's view on it, too. That bodybuilder called me "the racket" because I kept butting in and out when he was in the Green Room. I expected to find him copy-catting Mummy on the mat as well as Sally.

Well, if he didn't, Sally kept on at it as her daily routine.

I've rattled on, and I still haven't got to the horns of my dilemma about Sally. You had that problem with your mother after your father died and your mother was weathering the second-tier effects of senile dementia. If she were in either the sanatorium or at home, did she know where she was? Where should she be, and who should take care of her?

Sally, as I've told you, has been the same for a long time, fit for nothing. When she left school, she started reading books for the first time in her life. She carried one with her everywhere. Replacements for the little lamb, I suppose. Books thick enough to stop a rifle bullet. The Troubles had started for her too. Daddy was pressing her to take a job. He had something for her in the Agency. She grabbed a book the minute he said Agency, and her *peripatetic* studies got going. Daddy said she had started up her own private hedge school. She was always away off in the fields, supposedly studying. But you would have thought advertising was Sally's métier – in a sense, she'd been working all her life on a Wellesley Ad.

Besides, random quotations and slogans were winging about in her head by the time William and I got married. I felt sorry leaving her, what with Mummy and Daddy being so old. I suppose she was hiding behind any old sheaf of words that didn't say *I do.*

She made that speech at our reception in the Culloden Hotel, there, in Craigavad. "Love should not be selfish," it started. "We have a tankard in our house that Oliver Cromwell drank out of. I am not a puritan and I have shared it with a hundred boys I have known." It was a sort of boast. But no boy shared her. And everybody was terribly embarrassed at her performance. Her "I'm the better sister" speech.

You heard it, close up – you were a bridesmaid at the head table, but you never saw this and I never told you. There was the most mind-warping scene upstairs in the Culloden when I went to change. Sally came to help me off with the dress. We carried it to the bed between us and we left it there. We even had a laugh about it. Then, my nerves went to my bladder. I had to go to the bathroom. When I came out, Sally had hauled off her clothes and was standing by the window where the sun was shining in. She may even have tried on the dress that we said we had laid to rest.

I don't know. I was angry all over again, thanking God she hadn't decided to go downstairs like that, just to get attention. I grabbed her by the shoulders. I spun her round and somehow my hands shifted to her neck.

That made her positively radiant. She didn't even look at me, she stared in front of her as if she was gazing out of the window still. Or over the heads of the guests, and the hacked chicken bones on their plates, at the reception downstairs.

I even looked out the window. There were trees between the hotel and the next house, and I wasn't sure if she had been staring into the leaves, or up the Belfast Lough.

It lay down the hill, on the other side of Sydenham, where the airport was. The water looked like an extension of the runway. Planes flipped in and out, as unable as I to make up their mind if they should stay, or fly.

I stood there, rigid in my travelling suit.

I told her, "You realize I could kill you when you look like that." This brightened her up better than a mouthful of compliments, and immediately she was putting her dress back on.

She kept this look on her face, as if her nakedness in the window had been a secret destination tucked away from everybody. As if our wedding car with the cans and the carnations was part of a wild goose chase.

"I was just having a little time to myself in the window with the sun," she said, then she gave me a kiss.

Mad or mischievous, Tina? She wanted me angry because her sister's anger was like admiration. 'I dare you to ignore me,' that's Sally's way with other people.

Remember when you met her at the Royal Yacht Club in Bangor, she was talking to someone about Rosicrucians. She trotted out this huge word for a philosophical sect she hadn't a notion of. One of those times you were back visiting your parents and catching up with the yacht club bunch, buying Celtic silver and gold body ornaments for Harrods. You heard her say "Rosicrucians," didn't you, Tina? You reported how others of the great disconnected in Bangor were going to the Hare Krishnas and the Maharishi Gi, or the Rastafarians and doing dread-locks while they dodged in between the bullets and the bombs singing "peace and piss on Ian Paisley," and what not.

Sally joined the longest, least-known, most esoteric name in the pack and sat all winter posing in the Green Room. Daddy invited some of his junior managers down to take her out. Then, one night, he ran into that effete ex-B Special, Thomas Tallboy Slattery, in a camel hair coat, the one Mummy had brought home with her that time. By then, he was gun-running for the U.D.A or U.V.F. Daddy said the two of them, Sally and Slattery, the B-Special, twittered in multisyllables, like tiny birds that have the most complicated calls. They were a *splendiferous, phantasmagorical* pair, he said.

Sally and Slattery went out drinking, and they came back drunk. Then, this TiT Slattery appeared in the living room where Daddy was sleeping with his thumbs tucked into his braces. Daddy loved to sit like that – his self-made man, pencil-in-the-shirt-pocket look. Tommy Slattery shook Daddy. "Incredible," Slattery told him. He was still in his camel hair coat, raising his hands to the ceiling. "INCREDIBLE!"

When Daddy was properly awake and went into the Green Room, Sally was shining with baby oil and dripping it over the mat, like a lamp to overflowing. The smell of the oil and the grimace on her face made Daddy want to cry because she was like a small child again, a small baby hiccupping with colic.

Incredible.

She talked normally enough in the morning.

I've read these particular letters of Daddy's over and over. Daddy blamed himself for bringing Tommy Slattery home for his own amusement. Enough to laugh any parent into the grave. Poor Daddy. He couldn't say Mummy was one rotten tree falling and knocking down a good one. After all, I had turned out all right. I had stood up to it. It was two hollow trunks, not three, cracking each other open when they hit. That's what Daddy said. Sally got her problems from the Wellesleys, not her mother. Our mother was someone Daddy had recognized long ago as having the Wellesley style.

The empty Wellesleys. We were everything Slattery admired, Daddy believed, because Slattery's ambition was to go mad with eccentric ecstasy too.

When I wrote Daddy back, or when I wrote back to Daddy, funny how we switch the language round without noticing, when we live here. I said I wasn't so sure that he didn't want to be murdered. A bloody strange bird full of artificiality, like those painted targets at a fairground that go round and round, repeating the same silly music, setting themselves up for a pot shot.

Dinner, Tina. William is just in. He knows I'm writing to you. He says it's very friendly and therapeutic. He says to tell you he remembers your frowns when you're thinking and not to let them sink in too deep over this.

10:00 P.M. STILL THE 18TH.

I did see Sally when Mummy died.

She put up a show of grief, but I believe she was pleased because it gave her exclusive rights to the photograph. She wouldn't let Daddy put it away. Why should he? He never came into the Green Room anyway, and she never left it.

He hadn't the heart to fight her out of it, or to tell me until later. I offered to come back with the children to stay for a while, and while I was writing, asking this, he started to scold me for going into Gym. Didn't I have a brain in my body, and a knack for words? He made me angry, writing about that and not answering me. I suppose he was defraying his bitterness about Mummy and Sally.

What should I do if I took up the pen, I asked him. What would he do this time around? Write ad-copy, or be a reporter and write about the Troubles in Ulster and everywhere else? Or would he be like me – run, jump and smash tennis balls and show others how to do the same? In any case, I was married, settled down, wasn't I? With two boys, in a family beyond the complication of any more Wellesley women.

Then, he wrote to tell me he was proud of me. I was so sane it turned the old family ghosts in their graves. The Roundhead Wellesleys, the ones mad enough to come to Ireland in the first place with their good General, Cromwell. They put out propaganda, even then. Proclamations and pamphlets, with decrees and appeals to people, who couldn't read a word of it.

Pen and paper. William is moving exclusively into paper. Did I tell you all about that in my last letter? In case I didn't, the new computers and their printers eat a tree a minute. The future lies in paper, William says. From the length of this you probably agree. How many pages have I disposed of, and have I got any nearer to the nub of the matter, Tina?

I offered to stay again after we came over for Mummy's funeral. I told you that.

But you can't stay here with your children, not in this house, not in this country, not with this problem of ours. That was Daddy's new line now. How glad he was, or so he said, that I had escaped the crazy vanity that the Irish cherish. I should count myself lucky and stay on the other side of the Rockies. So little colour all about, in Ulster. Only drab grey and green – the people on occasion touched up with a bit of blood.

Then, there was something else very dotty that Daddy said about the beauty of our family piety. Stripping oneself before God was a Wellesley tradition, a legitimate puritan streak. But it had been planted among a race of embellishers.

For him the embellisher bit went into Wellesley ads. My anger at him almost choked me.

There's nothing pressing, except my sleep. I can't write any more now. William is reading a report on a report, or something. His glasses are on his forehead and he's looking through the door at me. Will I wave for you?

September the nineteenth. This next part will come re-corded on a tape wrapped in the rest of the letter, Tina. I realized I wasn't writing you anymore. I was talking to you, and I couldn't cope with the quotation marks and etceteras if I was to let you know who was saying what and so on.

"In any case, the more philosophical he was about the situation, the more Daddy was distancing himself from Sally and leaving her to her own devices. Same for me, Tina. The longer this letter gets, the farther I feel removed from her, but coping with her at the same time.

"When he died, Daddy had another twenty letters, not mailed. Sally piled them up and read them in the Green Room. What fascinated her, I suppose, must have been that the more he wrote about Mummy, the more he mixed her up with Sally. That was her victory.

"Did I get mentioned, even though they were addressed to me? Out of sight, out of mind. He apologized in the last letter. To me, that is. 'Forgive me for keeping you away,' he said.

"Daddy always talked two ways at once.

"…She was shuddering and shivering, sitting naked in front of the photograph in the Green Room, as thin as Mummy by the time they broke into the house and Mrs. Moir got back to me on the phone. I called the Helen's Bay barracks. Daddy had been dead for days. Pickled, the police told me when I got there and I talked to them in person. He probably died happy, but my sister! They say they are used to psychotic displays, and very few suicides these days. But my sister, I informed them, had killed herself trying to sit as naked and lovely as my mother in the photograph. Their reply to that? They wished all the killings in Ulster were about something as simple as wanting to take your clothes off.

"But wasn't that what it was all about? I wanted to scream. Mad, repressed expression. But I kept my temper when I said it.

"That struck them none too kindly.

"I took her in the car after that. I knew what I had to do. I drove the road round all those drumlins from Comber to Downpatrick. Cold cu-Cumber, Daddy used to call it when we passed it in the old days, headed for Newcastle and the Slieve Donard Hotel. Remember Miss Arthur's line for drumlins – 'Basket of eggs topography.'

"Sally still sat as she liked to, with the window down and her hair pouring into her mouth. Her hand kept dragging it off her tongue. Not so she could talk. She hadn't had a thing to say since I pushed her into her clothes.

"She had dresses and jeans and nothing in between. No suits, nothing to do a decent day's work in, or to make the trip. I got her a Chanel suit for a journey of an hour and a half.

"I put her away, Tina.

"The chief psychiatrist's chat about lessons, exercises, relaxations, made it sound like the Insane School for Young Ladies of Quality in Downpatrick.

"Mr. Barton, that was the man's name, he took us round. He was proud of his pastel walls and their 'therapeutic' potential. But he whisked her off after trying to get her to say something. Like a potted plant the cat had peed in — she must have given him a stinking look or said something under her breath that he heard.

"Four more days went by without a word out of her to me. I stayed in Newcastle and came every morning and afternoon. Then, she did say something. I suppose it was when she was sure I was worried enough to keep coming back.

"'I can't hear the seagulls,' was what she came out with.

"That hurt me. The sea was near enough. Seven miles.

"'You're in Downpatrick,' I explained to her. 'St. Patrick is buried close by, in Saul. We passed it when I drove you down.'

"'Why didn't you stop?' she asked me. 'We could have visited him.'

"'If you'd asked, I would have.'

"As soon as I said that, she began to strip and it sent me into a rage. I grabbed the belt to the jeans she was wearing, pulled it out and held it buckled to her neck. I started tightening it. But she was already smiling at the pain it must have caused her, consulting, somewhere inside herself again. I yelled at her and she went on, peeling off the clothes while I held her by the neck.

"At that point, I was either going to go on and strangle her or let her go on doing what she wanted to.

"I let her go.

"But why do it in Downpatrick? She wasn't in the Green Room – all the walls were pastel perfect. I supposed, in the end, it was a shrine near a shrine she was setting up for people to come and pay homage at. Old St. Pat in Saul had taken over from Mummy on the wall. The two of them, living out their passion for divine revelation.

"Which doesn't reduce my guilt or my problem at all. She could stay there forever, in 'dementia praecox,' as the shrink of the pastel walls says his colleagues used to call it. But Tina, could I have brought her out to the West Coast?

"What Saints are there for me to tell her about in the Pacific Northwest? Who could give her the sacred admiration she needs. She would be just another dazed blonde, a beached log, but sinking in her madness beside girls who could still bob about, even if every man on the West Coast ran in and out of them like the tide.

"But perhaps I'm cruel and unkind to the girls here. Let me know soon, Tina. Let me know.

"Gerry."

THE DARK BARBER

Maybe it's the damaged leg crooked in our direction, his knee nudging my thigh as he does the back-and-sides that gives him this combat stance. Maybe 'cause he's short he has to thrust his scissors up, or if down – like, it's from his tippy-toes, and that seems to turn those scissors into scimitars and Afran into an assassin, not a bona fide barber. Or it's his thunderhead of hair, sharp jaw, eyes daring every male on the street to come in for the fricassee of his scissors that keeps them all from finding out.

"He's incredible," I say to his partner. Other customers, sitting and waiting for the partner, might take what I say as a promo for the impaired. But my hair *is* thicker. What I call my UFO – the shiny, balding disc of white skin that floats on top of my head, the tonsure I bear, like some sorry monk's – shrinks under the blades.

"If you like him, it happen," says his Libyan partner and the Kurd grins. But do any of those going bald, who need his cut and follicular fill-up, see it? They stick their noses in their tabloid, like it has men's perfume in the print.

And so, for many moons, like wee boys my neighbour, Billy, and fellow agers squirm in their chairs and their unease always undoes what Afran, the Kurd, conjures. Then, they don't like how he retreats to his cubby hole at the back of the barber shop, pulls a curtain across and mumbles in what must be Kurdish, or he goes on in his stammering and staggering English. There is a computer, a monitor, an office chair in there, and a Persian mat (it's not big enough to be a carpet) on the floor. Enough to take his knees, if he prays on it. Often as not, when he pulls back the curtain to come out, he has left a plastic container rimmed with the remains of his lunch on top of the monitor. Like a silly upside-down hat with a creamy fringe at the bottom.

At the end of the day, he takes off his white barber's jacket and puts on a padded black bomber to go home. On his way to the bus stop, he pulls open the flap to the night safe at the Royal Bank. Holding the flap, his head bobs a few times as if he communes with the depository or addresses doubts about dropping the day's take into its chute. Then, he crosses the road and boards the 99 Express across town. No, he doesn't kneel and whizz home on his tiny prayer mat, but the 99 Express slices through the city, west to east.

Since I pay him this much attention, and because I let him cut my hair, other customers keep asking me what's he up to behind the curtain. As if letting him cut my hair has made me intimate with every mumble that exits his mouth in his little retreat. But being Moslem, would his little place be called a retreat, and having no idea what it means, my neighbour, Billy Barlow, declares it to be a *haj*, a hell hole.

"He's calling him again," Billy tells me, when Afran's voice comes through the curtain, clear as sanded glass his voice comes in, "Yes, yes, stop loss, twelff dollars and sixty sens!"

Billy elbows me. "Twelve bucks and sixty cents…" Billy's a Shop teacher and has chisels for elbows. "Twelve bucks and sixty cents – what for?"

I elbow Billy Barlow back.

"Extra payment. To stop customers losing their hair after he cuts it?"

Billy gives a guffaw, followed by a gurgle as he swallows his gob of mockery. "Are you serious?"

In the hot, late-summer afternoon, only three of us are in the shop. Billy and me, waiting, and the one up for the Libyan, who squirms as he listens to us. I get up and go to the curtain to ask Afran how long he will be, and there's Afran, hunched forward in his chair, prayerfully, or like he's passing a kidney stone, nodding and talking to his cell phone.

"Please, I talk business to my broker."

The curtain whips back into place.

"Kurds, very special," says the Libyan to the back of his customer's head. "Kurds and business, like chicken and egg, always hatch this or that. But Afran special, he have *djinn*."

"Gin sling, cotton gin?" Billy badgers.

The Libyan partner eyeballs Billy. "His *djinn*! You like him, more hair. You not, bit maybe fall out." Second eyeball job on neighbour Billy. "Which you like grow, money or you' hair?" (What's the Libyan implying, Afran offers a choice?) Then, he turns from Billy and myself to watch the soccer on the TV, set high on a bracket in the window corner, above the window box, where cacti lean west to the setting sun.

Can Afran apply his *djinn* to the stock market, where human emotions and the fundamentals bash each other up and down, like Punch and Judy? On the same formula, 'You like it, it grow,' Afran's key to needing less custom. As if reading my mind, the Libyan comes back to Afran. "North of the Kirkuk, Afran learn make things grow of nothing. Some dirt, some water, like Allah make man of nothing."

"Aha," says I, "he's a farmer who became a barber."

The client in the chair gives the Libyan a hard look, wanting him back at work on his short back and sides.

I'd love to give him a kick in the back and sides for shutting off the info on Afran.

As it is, I'm left to mull over those growths that aren't cancer and watch Billy plant his feet on the metal footrest, like Butch Cassidy mounting his horse. I have had my own encounters with inexplicable growth. Like Billy, I planted my feet down once, but on the floor, wrestling with a green, wool cardigan my mother knit me. I yelled at its fake, Aran-island ribs for it to quit growing on me. Crazily, it grew, like the sheep was still alive in the wool. When it reached my knees, my mother cut it back up to my hips. Again and again, till I was too spooked to wear her gift that kept growing. I took it on a hike and threw it in a field. I screamed at it to go graze till its buttons turned back to cloven hooves. But was it me who brought the wool to life in the ugly cardigan? No way. The thing in the tips of my ma's knitting needles, same thing as in Afran's scissors, did the trick. Though Afran doesn't swamp and smother me with his prodigious gift, like my mother.

"Does he go back?" I ask the Libyan, who works on Billy Barlow's hair, top of the head, like it's inches higher than it is. I haven't been back in two years to see my mother in Ireland and I ask the Libyan out of guilt.

"He-can-not-go-back," the Libyan says, each syllable timed to a snip at Billy Barlow's hair. Billy's eyes roll, but mine narrow.

"Afran No. 1 Baghdad barber. You see Saddam hair, thick black bear hair. Afran, Saddam barber."

"What?" Billy almost stabs his face on the Libyan's scissors. "And you were Muammar Gaddafi's!"

The Libyan gives Billy a bow, "But Afran *djinn*...poor Afran *djinn*."

"What about it?" Billy asks.

"Other side of head – tail. You not like him, hair not grow; *he* not like *you*, hair stop grow."

"What's that got to do with him and Saddam?'

"Afran, like Saddam money. Not like Saddam. Soon as Afran see Saddam thin spot, he flee north to the Kirkuk."

"And?"

"Saddam send army find his barber."

"Did Afran have a wife and kids there?" I ask.

"Whole fam'ly. North of the Kirkuk. Safer than Baghdad City."

"Did the army find him?"

"Saddam army break down door. Rifle break Afran hip, here," the Libyan points to the breakage point. "Knee, there." He taps his right knee, on what we know to be the leg in question, the one that swings before it lands on the other side of the barber's chair and customer's head.

A voice from beyond the curtain, "I tell them when my hurt heal. I go back Baghdad," and still talking, Afran adds, "Okay. At market, for the Honeywells."

The Libyan holds his scissor-free hand on Billy's head, "That when Afran flee and that when Saddam gas his Kurdish people. Halabja."

"Jesus," says Billy. "All over a barber who wouldn't do his hair!"

"Billy, for God's sake, didn't you read about it?"

"I run and my family die without me," voice from behind the curtain again.

Billy sticks out his leg and taps it. "Run?"

A sound follows, like a dull spit hitting a carpet – correction, Afran's prayer mat, clearly visible when he snaps back the curtain and steps out. "I escape on truck. Truck driver, uncle of my wife. He take me through Kurdish country, into Turkey."

After that, limping emphatically, he waves us out. Billy, with his hair half cut.

"End of trading for today!" he tells us.

Afran makes me ashamed of my pettiness, the way I ran away from my country. Belittling the wool of an old cardigan, knitted with love, blaming it for smothering me in that love. I never truly recognized my mother's loneliness that went into the wool for that cardigan after my father died. Now, I feel the full length of Afran's loneliness, passing into my impoverished locks, causing them to fill the emptiness on my head the way he wishes the emptiness in his to be covered with the kisses of his wife and children.

On the short way back to our block, Billy Barlow wants to know if I believe all that BS.

"Every bit," I reply.

"The sob story – to have me pick the Kurd, out of pity for the poor turd?"

"Don't diss the guy, Billy. Kurds got history. Pulled across borders by Iraqis, Syrians, Iranians, pulled apart like Christmas crackers. But Kurds got these talents. Believe me, unbelievable talents."

Billy tells me the only thing he believes unbelievable are my wife's delphiniums in the front garden.

I can't deny it. They tower over everything else, her blue Babylons of delphinium.

Still, visit after visit, I continue my watch, to see if squirmers lose more than they pay for. Some do go to Afran, those in a hurry, who can't wait for the Libyan. I talk to them, and true, but paradoxical – the finer the fringe, the more balding, the sooner the visit. So, I soon see them back to ask if they like Afran, but they never answer, and I can't tell normally receding hair from hexed.

No matter. Where my own fairy ring of flesh, that hallowed circle, used to shine, I've got a bristly thatch, a bit of Brad Pitt, which my wife says is a damn implant and promptly pores over the VISA bills and medical statements from our extended coverage. She has some reservations about my mother and the upcoming trip to Ireland.

Again, when the barber shop is empty and Afran in consultation with his broker or watching the business channel on his monitor, placing his mug of coffee on top of it, like a crown, I ask the partner, "Can't you tell more people?"

"Tell? They think he crazy. And piss off customer coming. Guy in chair that day, not Mr. Barlow guy, that other guy, never come back. And Mr. Barlow think I am bit nuts for what I say already."

I am still obsessed with unaccountable growth, and I wonder, besides Afran's trims that trigger it, what else around and about me grows that fast after it's cut, well, apart from the grass, or wool on that nutty green cardigan. Those poppies! A bunch, the landlords of a rented house across our lane cut from the front lawn and threw onto the rubbish heap at the back. They reseeded real quick. I don't know if they're the heroin bearing kind that fill the fields in Kurdish Turkey, Kurdish Iraq or Afghanistan, but they get looked at on the heap, as if they belong to an obnoxious grow-op. Same look as Afran gets through the shop window.

Just to show I have no objections to them in the lane, that I actually like their rabid, exotic growth, I put down my nose to test for scent, but those poppies have none, or my nose is no good. Very likely, judging by what happens when Afran's scissors come up for my nose hairs. If they're aimed up there for me to sniff some growth-crazy chlorophyll, I smell only antiseptic wash from the vase, where Afran plants the scissors. Then, the lobes for the finger holes just gape out of it, like empty metal petals.

But I'm not disappointed. Forty of us regulars are now in the know, a select believer-group under the balding scrutiny of the dumb majority. On his behalf we swear he'd not harm a hair on anybody's head. The very opposite, his scissors sow what they snip, and we boys in the know bow our heads to bear witness to our peers in the barber shop.

LONELY RIVERS FLOW TO THE SEA, TO THE SEA, TO THE OPEN ARMS OF THE SEA

Don Mateo sings this song, or mournfully hums under the lyrics passing through his mind for "Unchained Melody." Even though he doesn't understand the English floating underneath the singer's voice and across the landscape in the movie he loved and saw ten times with the subtitles to guide him, he sings until everybody around him in the Cine Cuautla yells at him to shut the singing or they'll shoot him.

He sings it as he crosses the aqueduct, fed by the *apantle* a few miles away. He loves the sound of this instant river that erupts from the earth, out of a mound heaped with *epazote*, cilantro, watercress and everything green that clings to a well-watered place, especially the banks and ditches that follow the *apantle* along the side of the cane fields until it reaches the stone aqueduct. The aqueduct sprouts thick walls on either side for the *apantle*, providing a narrow conduit for the water to pass through. It crosses twenty metres in the air, over a great dip in the earth to rush like applause into a hamlet on the other side.

As a boy, Don Mateo sat in the aqueduct, holding onto the stone walls on either side with his forearms, letting the water build up behind until it reached his ears and the force shot him across the length of the aqueduct. Strong as a breaker from the ocean, smashing out of its confinement, banging him from side to side, skinning his elbows, while he closed his eyes and imagined he *was* in the ocean far away where the water from the *apantle* went.

Walking home with his machete from his day's work in the cane fields, he imagines he keeps the *apantle* company on part of its long course toward the ocean. He can hear its distant crash in the rush of the aqueduct as he crosses on one of the stone walls used for going into town. Cuautlenses pass on the other side and greet him, going out.

He doesn't live in Cuautla, he lives on a shrunken *milpa* over the other side of the Pan American Highway, where it climbs the slope out of Cuautla toward Azúcar de Matamoros and the new *Panteón*. There, he will be buried because the old one, which is much closer to his home, lies filled to the brim. If he turned into a cicada or a firefly, he could take up residence in the trees above the old *Panteón* and hurtle past his sons and grandsons, daughters and granddaughters like a green grenade, lobbed out of their family's long history of dying in this town, which he has never left for the ocean. No, not once, although he is certain the *apantle* reaches it on his behalf, joining up with other comrade waters for companionship on the journey.

He sings about the lonely rivers until he reaches the *pulquería*, where he stops every night after quitting the cane fields. In the *pulquería*, he releases his hooked machete and sets it along the side of the table. The *pulquero* behind the serving hatch dips his head to look and check who he is. The *pulquero* nods his head at the machete, turns his head to the side like a bird while pursing his lips into a beak, as if trying to work out if the machete is set there for convenience or for business.

How many years has he looked through that hatch at Don Mateo the same way?

If Don Mateo sat with the machete dangling at his side, it might trip someone passing, or bother him by bumping on the floor every time he moved, or knock against him on his way to the lavatory – even swing in front of his fine flow of yellow piss. No one will steal it. Not with square eyes behind the hatch keeping an eye on all the machetes laid as carefully as cutlery on the sides of the tables. Too many machetes, too confusing for a thief to take a pick.

Fausto, a much-younger relative, shuffles in and sits down opposite Don Mateo with his back to the hatch, where he will go to order his mug of *pulque* and one for Don Mateo. Fausto doesn't like to see the *pulquero's* face and the look that says, ah ha, Fausto has to sit with Don Mateo whether he likes it or not.

As a nephew, his sister's son, with more great-nephews for Don Mateo on the way, he needs Don Mateo's permission to add to the small building space Don Mateo has allotted him on Don Mateo's *milpa*. Fausto feels crowded in his little home, crowded in the *pulquería,* and that is what galls him every night when, at some juncture, Don Mateo tells him about how listening to the *apantle* makes him feel free because it flows all the way to the sea.

Every night, sure as the fifth mug of *pulque*, Don Mateo will say, "God bless the god Quetzalcoatl for inventing this *pulque*. Down through the ages it pours to us, just like our *apantle* to the sea."

His nephew, Fausto, knows Don Mateo has worked on this salute to *pulque* and to the *apantle* for years before he got the right words, almost as many years, months and days as Fausto has waited for permission on the extension. But Don Mateo gets drunk, forgets, falls into bed after Fausto carries him home and drops him into it. Then, when his uncle wakes up, he thinks it is the same day as the day before.

Fausto's aunt, Doña Celestina has begged Fausto to be in the *pulquería* for when he must carry Don Mateo home across the highway.

Fausto wants to know why Don Mateo doesn't use his mangy horse. Except Fausto would have to be there to shove him into the saddle. His uncle doesn't let him add-on because he knows Fausto would have no call to be here at his beck and call any more, ready to heave him over his shoulder.

"Uncle, please, let me add-on."

The fifth mug gavels the table as Don Mateo lands it with relish. "Quetzalcoatl will be pleased. Add-on as much as you please in his praise."

"Jesus," says Fausto, "you don't hear, do you, *Tío* Mateo!"

"What don't I hear?"

Fausto stomps over to the hatch and buys himself the biggest mug of *pulque* he can get and doesn't bring a matching one for Don Mateo.

"To the god whoever," says Fausto and drinks it, then goes for another, which goes down just as brazenly in front of his uncle. Then, Fausto stands and declares, "The *apantle* goes into a river that ends up in a lake. Didn't you ever hear that in school?"

"I never went to school, as you know, and I hear what the *apantle* tells me. The *apantle* tells me it goes all the way to the sea with its friends.

"No, it does not."

Don Mateo stands, reaches across the table and slaps Fausto across the face.

Fausto jumps up and before he knows what he has done, he has picked up his machete and swept the ear from the side of Don Mateo's head.

"See what you hear now!"

He has just come out with a bitter oxymoron, but Fausto is much to blame for the long, long wait and his wrath because, a while ago, Fausto had a scheme for paying Don Mateo for his add-on.

Fausto's brother-in-law, Fidel, nearly drowned in the *apantle* when he was baptized by the pastor from the Baptist church. Fidel has land. The near-drowning to save his soul didn't stop Fidel from signing up for Bible College, so he could do unto others as the pastor had done to him.

Fidel owned one big field in particular, which Fausto could rent for a song or a hymn, which he practises with his brother-in-law, for when he fulfilled a promise to be the first soul Fidel will dunk in the *apantle* and save for Jesus. These watery conversions take place close by the Baptist church, shortly after the water gushes out of the aqueduct, hence the perilous footing for the baptizer and the about-to-be baptized.

Don Mateo liked the story of Fidel very, very much.

"I'd die to be born again as a boy in the *apantle*."

"You'd be born again as a Baptist, *Tío* Mateo, but I have a better way for us to follow Fidel, by planting onions and tomatoes in his big field. That's where Fidel made his money."

"Tell me more, and tell me why your brother-in-law, Fidel, doesn't want to make that money anymore."

"He will collect it by the bucketful when he is a pastor. I have seen it with my own eyes, big plastic buckets full of pesos every Sunday."

"So, how do we find the time to work Fidel's field?"

"We don't cut cane for one planting and plant onions in Fidel's field instead. The money we make will pay you for the use of your land and cover the cost of the add-on for my tiny wee house. The older kids can't bear listening to us at night, eating, arguing, and you know what in the same room."

"Very well," said Don Mateo, but he should have known better.

The rain baptized that field continually in the season when there was supposed to be no rain. Fidel had regular irrigation from the *apantle* that ran on his side of town, all the water he needed and all the sunshine through the dry season. But that accursed *apantle* ran past the *Barrio Rojo*, then under the Pan American, to Fidel's field. It slunk between the dingy whore-huts, where the harlots of Cuautla set up business after pious President Miguel de la Madrid tossed them out of their lovely, well-lit, lively, old street behind La Paz Convent School. You could dance in the big cantinas with your choice or sit and have a tête-à-tête at a table or tit-to-tit in a booth at one of the lounge bordello bars.

Testing the waters for his onions, Fausto tasted that godforsaken *apantle*, face down, lucky not to be knifed, only relieved of the money for their plantings in his loose cotton trousers, the money for the first load they were to put in.

As if to punish Fausto for his sins, the unseasonal rains surged down on the unlucky onions, sunk to their tufted tops in mud. After which, for trying to trick God, Jesus and Fidel the Baptist brother-in-law, Don Mateo dubs Fausto a rotten onion. Did Fausto not know that John, the first in the line of the Baptists, damned the adultery and harlotry of the Hebrews?

"It happens in the best of families," the *pulquero*'s wife tells Don Mateo in the car as she takes him out onto the highway, down the slope and across the bridge over the river that the *apantle* flows into, not a stone's throw from the Seguro Social Hospital.

Don Mateo sits in the front seat, holding his ear in his hand. Every so often he holds it back up to where it belongs. He would not let them wrap it in a cotton cloth. His face wrinkles up in agony from the wound, or he is listening very profoundly to whatever he hears when he returns his ear to its original place.

Fausto sits in the back with his head in his hands.

"What will I tell *Tía* Celestina?"

"Tell her you wanted to slap him on the shoulder, like – for a good joke, and you missed."

"With a machete?"

"I've seen it done. Like those *Ingleses* make somebody a knight for a good deed, why not for a good joke."

The *pulquero*'s wife talks, believing Don Mateo can't hear the half of it because of his mutilation. Distress also makes her silly, she can't help it.

Fausto can't believe his ears.

The one doctor surgeon on late call can't believe that Don Mateo doesn't want his ear sewn back on.

"*Por Dios, hombre*, it will be as good as new. It's like just a shell, it contours sound into the ear. It's the gristly ear lug, not the actual hearing part of the ear."

The surgeon should have kept his mouth shut.

"Like a shell."

"Yes."

"And shells can hear the sea?"

"People believe you put a shell to your ear and you can hear the waves of the sea come in and out, but it is only the blood going through your head, pumped through there in waves by your heartbeats. Don Mateo."

"I don't think so."

"Sterilize and put a dressing on it, Doctor. Do as Don Mateo says. Don Mateo is the owner of Don Mateo's bits and pieces, attached or detached," says the nurse, nodding at Fausto, who sits disconsolately in a chair. The nurse is a second cousin, Fausto's wife is her *criada* and has been serving her richer side of the family since childhood.

Months pass. Don Mateo's ear dries into a relic of the ruction in the *pulquería*, but he brings it with him everywhere, and takes it out like others take a watch in the breast pocked from the end of a chain. He joins people with Doña Celestina in the Hotel Santa Cecelia where people of that watch-in-breast-pocket calibre would dine on a Sunday, if there were any left. All the men dress in *guayabera* and wear wrist watches. None raise them to their ear to check the tick of the chronometry.

Don Mateo and Doña Celestina are being treated by Fausto and his wife. They note the huge graphic of Don Quijote and Sancho Panza on the inside gable end of the dining room, the knight's raggedy body and clothing swirling up to the curved ceiling beside the bold black blob and blur of Panza.

An architect owns the hotel and another in Acapulco. His son-in-law manages both and flits between one and the other, avoiding the tax collectors, who have been known to come with a van to remove televisions, fridges, for those unpaid. Acting like a pawnbroker until the items are redeemed for cash.

But the architect's son-in-law knows languages and the ocean. He speaks French, English and rumoured to spout Japanese and Chinese. He brings an informed opinion unlike his nephew, Fausto, or his wife or anyone Don Mateo has spoken to on the matter.

When Don Mateo spots him coming in for a cursory inspection of the diners and the service, Don Mateo darts forward and pulls at the tail of his *guayabera*.

"I am told you know Cuautla and you know Acapulco and the ocean very well. May I ask you a question?"

"A customer can always ask me a question."

"Does our *apantle* that crosses the aqueduct and enters the river go to the sea?"

"The customer is always right and in this case you are actually, yes, I'm sure of it, right."

"Now will you please tell me what you hear?"

Don Mateo removes his ear from the pocket of his grey *guayabera*, which matches the crustaceous pallor of the ear. He puts it to his good ear, nods, then holds it out for the manager to do the same, which he does, holding it just out of contact with his own

"What do you hear?"

Seeing Don Mateo's eagerness and being familiar with Acapulco and what goes on there, having heard the French-Canadian, the Anglo-Canadian and out-and-out gringo, he can understand what is required of him with this question about the sea and what he hears there.

"I hear waves and voices."

"What did I tell you?" Don Mateo shouts back at the lowered heads around his table. "Waves and voices!"

The manager puts his head to the side, like a bird, puckering his lips and his brow, appearing to hear a lot more in Don Mateo's ear.

"They are speaking a very funny French and a very funny English."

Don Mateo takes possession of his ear again and plops it back into his pocket like a watch that has told the right time of day. He has what he wants, confirmation.

His ear proves it.

TENNIS

They tell me, report nothing, Gene. That how they say Jean. Report nothing or they think you the one involved, and you become the suspect. You try help this guy, broken up in some accident, and they sue you for fix him up. Like, even if you are an MD surgeon – you keep out, or else you spend your holiday in the police station, making the statement. Somebody sue the boots off your feet, and you go no place.

Something about a bad dose of Napoleonic Law Mexicans got. We have the good recipe for it in Québec, but here, the Napoleonic Law sort of got the shits. Like from the fruit, too much heat.

That what I think about the run-over guy. Don't look up close. And I think, why the car not make it over his head? An auto leave a big impression on a guy's head. Like cat you see on the highway – flat. Like pizza with the hair topping. But this head is still one piece and the res' – neck, ches', knee, an' his ankle – run over.

Damn taxi-driver stop for nothing, I think. They jus' run him over, one after the other. Too busy to make the stop in case they miss the next fare. This too much, I tell Rose-

Marie. I pull him up, I put him against the door of that *Club de Tenís*.

From Adam, I don't know this one guy. But me, I feel sad for him, and the love charm he have on his gold bracelet. I know it.

Since we been in Acapulco, we are buying pretty heavy. We work hard for the good deal in silver or gold off the beach vendor. Make the bid, wait one day or two, see it drop. Anyway, I watch the jewellery and I ask people what price and where they buying. I remember the good jewellery, and I know it on the guy. For sure, because you know, I see his partner put that there gold bracelet on the wrist of that run-over guy.

This late night – 11 p.m. The Shore Patrol from the Hornos base, they come, and they are stepping into the gateway and into the doorway. They go look-see, like the garbage men in Montréal. Then, the run-over guy, he say, "Vamoose," like they do in the movie. Rose-Marie and I figure they must be two sailor, who sneak in the *Club de Tenís* for some back and forth with the ball – and the bracelet, it for some bet what the one guy win.

"Two handsome guy," say Rose-Marie, "and that bracelet with the love charm heart look pretty good to this old bird."

Morning and afternoon, lotsa women go in there, to the *Club de Tenís*. Handsome, well-preserve' women like Rose-Marie. When the limo leave them, they show a lot of the leg in white short. Lot of brown Mexican leg. It make you want to hit that furry ball, whip that feather birdie all day. This what one of the two sailor is twirl – white cork head of that feather birdie wit' his finger. And while one is kissing his bracelet with the love charm heart – this other sailor is suck the cork on his birdie.

I touch this here lucky charm that he kiss, but Rose-Marie is giving me the instruction, "Jean Rubinsky, the police," and "Jean Rubinsky, the ambulance;" and I say, "I take no gold heart off this sailor." I touch his lucky charm like I say sorry for you, sailor; I sure would like to know you better. An' I wan' tell him some thing – like I know you are one cute guy, an' my Rose-Marie not mind to have you in her bed. But, I sure as hell glad some taxi make the pizza out of you first.

Now, Rose-Marie, she want me to telephone. "Jean, you make the report to this Mr. Tiger. Jean, you can tell it to him in French, tell him in the English. Jean, in Mexican, like it say in the paper.' Now, Rose-Marie read it and I read it in the *Montreal Magazine,* about this Hot-Dog-Eater Chief of Police. Ex-Mountie, Manitoba, then Montréal, then Aca-pulco. He say Montréal get too crazy with the violence, and why just be the constable or sergeant in Montréal when he qualify for Chief and get more pay for give the criminals target practice in Acapulco.

And on top, he have family here in Acapulco, and he have this licence from the UNAM. Some guy tell me it the Mexico University, not United Nations, and I think – the Hot-Dog-Eater is educated man. He listen. He know I got no beef with this road accident. I take no bracelet. I take a look is all – jus' make sure the guy is the one I see kissing the other guy before Hornos Shore Patrol catch them. Big Mexican *abrazo* – each guy suck the other up, like two Pepsi on one hot-damn day.

"But this run-over guy still got his wallet," I tell Rose-Marie. "This mean he is jus' run-over. Not no victim in no robbery."

"Ah-oui," Rose-Marie, she yell at me – *"ne touches pas ça!"*

Okay, I got my fingerprint on the dead sailor wallet. I rub them off, but that when I remember what like I see from the corridor back of our room. I waiting for Rose-Marie to finish fix the hair. That corridor got windows that look inland and I got my big glasses that can see all the way to Japan.

It morning and the *Club de Tenís* get lotsa light from the east and I see the run-over sailor and this other sailor wrestle in their tennis short. On the tennis court – on the roof, they do like that lambada. One of them get the other from behind and he hold him. Hand in his pant, for squeeze him, like kids do when they play like they are mad at each other. Except Rose-Marie, she tell me, now that she have a good look, now that she have the hair combed out of her eye, *"Ils sont fou d'amour,"* crazy in love.

Two ladies come out, start play, make pretty shot. They bend for pick up the ball and look at them two sailor, to watch see a smile at their nice move with that bat and the ball. Now, those guy are off each other back. And, the two sailor boy smile at the women like the women are the ice cream and their tongue keep one special lick for them.

Then, I remember I see the run-over guy, one night, at the *Club de Tenís*. He shove out the door. He rock up and down on the *Club de Tenís* sidewalk, which is all wreck with the truck and with the taxi. The sailor boy slip, and he turn, yell good and loud at this ol' man in this Mexican shirt. You know them silk shirt, like jacket with pockets. That old guy, he hold that other shipmate – his sailor friend, he hold him by the arm. He say, "*Puto, no tokay.*" Then, he yell, "*No tokay o te mato.*"

'*Tokay, te mato,*' that what he say. He as mad as Rose-Marie when I touch the wallet to find this run-over guy name.

I confess. I got this one habit. I sneak big sundowner before Rose-Marie finish the siesta. I go to the lobby, talk to the porter, then I go down the street see what new at the *Club de Tenís*. That when I see the old guy.

One of the Anglos at La Copa and me, we watch that mêlée between this angry old guy and those two sailor. Anglo tell me, "You find those fags, fucked to death at your feet, don't interfere! That there is a love triangle. Old gentleman there is keeping that young one he's got by the arm and he is pissed at his new playmate. Mexicans fix problems like that with guns. Don't interfere."

"Me," I say. "One guy be eating the balls of the other guy on a plate, and all I say is bon appétit!"

But Rose-Marie say I nosier than her mother. 'Fact, her mother love me more than Rose-Marie for I got all this stuff to tell.

The old guy I see one, maybe two time more. He have the condo down this street by the beach. I see him drive in, Friday, 8 p.m., then, Monday, 7 – 'e drive out same. Same thing nex' Friday an' Monday.

You bet I watch. Giving the eyeball a refill with jus' sunshine get boring, if you got one month to kill. You bet I get to watch this street like it my neighbourhood.

This old guy, he got his condo so he be near the big naval base. Anyway, that time in the street, when they play the love triangle. It a real ding-dong match. The old guy take the black ball for the squash. He squeeze his thumb in it, and he flick it in the face of the run-over guy. He take the birdie thing and he squish it on the run-over guy head.

But the run-over guy, he too flat and bad beat-up for that birdie or some ping-pong bat to be the murder weapon.

Anyway, we go get taxi and tell this Mister Tiger guy. We tell him what I tell you, Clement. Them Mexican at the desk lick up our French, like it ice cream, but they talk English back. The Acapulco Mountie, he talk French good, and he talk it until we go back and we see this *cadaver* with all the Mexican cop in Acapuko stare at it. Then, he not talk, he say nothing in Mexican or English.

"*Merci,*" he say for the statement, "*merci,*" for the old guy description. For the condo informations, the informations about the birdie and squash ball that the ol' guy squeeze. "*Merci. J'aime le Québec, c'est pour les raisons de famille que je suis de retour au Mexique.*"

He say all this in French, like he talk to himself. He has this wife, a Mexican woman, and her family not like the police – detective of the police, no better. She think Mexican police are the criminals, he say. He say he tell her we go to Canada where the police have respect, and he study, and he work so he can make RCMP, but the wife, she stay in Mexico with the son. See what happen to him, Mr. Tiger, in *le Canada*, first.

Next thing, he tell me she say she divorce him. So, he come down for get back the respect of his son. And he still pay so his wife can eat *les petit-fours*, *les entrecôtes*. Now, he say, I will see you and Rose-Marie to your hotel, Jean, and you will have the protection of my department.

"Why we need the protection?" Rose-Marie ask. And when she see the big tear in Mr. Tiger eye, she think it because the Hot-Dog-Eater not be able to protect us. We are in some hot shit.

"We stop go out late. If we lose the nightlife, we are having the pleasure of the morning. Firs' light – up. But morning is good time to make the hit. No people. Only fishermens in the boat that pull in the net. And any assassin follow our footprint, easy – in the sand. I tell Rose-Marie so every time we walk over where the little guy from the hotel rake the san'. "But this is dumb, Jean," Rose-Marie say. "Other people out for the walk mix up their mark with our mark in the sand."

Rose-Marie pretend she is the brave one, but for two, three day we are real scared. Everything look bigger than I ever see it. We see this small hairy fish that got big head and whisker like Rose-Marie *maman*. Fat head you can't tell from the body, with the big cut 'cross it, like some speedboat hit it good with the propeller. I see the sun make the hair stick out on Rose-Marie face. Québec women sure have the bristle. They take the electrolysis for kill the hair on their faces, an' they don't show moustache. If we get back, I make that the present for Rose-Marie. But we see no cop, no criminal no place, but how we tell undercover cop from criminal?

When fish boats come in, chef from the bistros go pick in the boat for the good fish. They make the bargain. This morning we see the demonstration at this boat that lie way up on the sand. We say, for sure – they buy the fish. Only the other guys, the Shore-Patrol guys, they come. They are looking for the sailor that get drunk and not make it back to base. They look under the boat for them, like the people from the bistro look for the fish, inside.

Or Shore Patrol buy fish this morning, 'cause they bored for not find guys go AWOL. For now they are poke in the boat with *les chefs* bistro. And me, I got the blister on my bare feet from the tough brown sand here and I am real glad to make the stop. I don't know what the matter with that sand. Maybe the sea make her too quick and not grind her up right.

"Jean, dépêche-toi," Rose-Marie say when she see the feet that stick out of that boat. Feet that are cover in one big cake of this crazy ginger sand.

Rose-Marie, she have the front row. "Jean, this the other, the not run-over guy," she shout at me. "Jean, Jean," she shout.

One big argument go on with the Shore Patrol and the guy who own that boat. The Shore Patrol point at what in the dead guy mouth, what stick out with the wet feather. Sure this thing have feather, but for sure is no seagull. The Shore Patrol, they pull it out and the top is turn brown with the blood, like end of hot dog I dip in the ketchup.

Rose-Marie, she choke, but she say, "See." And all those guys see loud and clear.

But *Acapulco Times* say it is this:

The son of Police Chief Tigre and the son of the Mayor of Igualada have been found dead two days apart. Both were doing their military service at Hornos base and both were able-bodied seamen. Although recent elections in Guerrero have recorded fewer murders, these deaths are considered political and designed as warnings for the Mayor and Chief of Police, who are known to be independents and who stop at nothing to see justice done. The Mayor was not available for comment, and when interviewed, Alonso Tigre said that all kinds of love speak their name in Mexico nowadays, but the one that must bite its lip is the love of freedom and fair play. My loss is your loss that is how democracy works. A crime committed by one is like a mistake made by all.

We got all kinds of stuff in Québec. We keep what we seen from the Mexico reporters. I tell you, Clement, this what happen. It no love triangle, like the Anglo say. This what I learn in geometry, long time ago. This is love quadrangle, for these two sons and two poppas square off. You get the big picture, Clement? Guys who got sons gotta be the policeman nowadays.

After it all over, we still got two week and *Noel.*. We have the Christmas turkey in the Copacabango. But out there on the big deck with all that water rush at the hotel, turkey that the chef carve not look right size. It shrink or something. We don't know. Rose-Marie and me, we don't like eat turkey outdoor. The fresh pineapple, cut up, is better. It look jus' right.

CUP-W

What's wrong with me is I never had anybody like her to paint the way for me, make sure I didn't do dumb stuff that would hurt. I bin pretty active in CUP-W and done crazy stuff on the picket line. What do I care if I ain't married, I got CUP-W to keep me warm. Okay. CUP-W is like the size of the Union bra, but if I had somebody like her, I wouldn't complain if I had to deliver her bikinis to the dry cleaners every day. But material like that isn't machine washable. I'd do them by hand. That shows you how lonely I get in that apartment of mine near the river there, in Hull. I quit drooling over what women got in their undies and start thinking about what a good wash I could do for them. Any woman's smell's gotta be better than them ball-huggers and socks of mine, especially after I've stood through the weigh-ins of the morning mail at the delivery bay.

Another sign you're gettin' old, when you remember the price of your underwear, what percentage of polyester you got in your shirts, how much wool there is in your socks like it was part of your union contract. I got this thing against material that shrinks now, like it's life-threatening. My damn skin, the poor stuff is thinning and wrinkling all over me too.

Now her. That cloth she's got makes her bikinis fit perfect. Then, maybe it's that perfect body she's got that holds them on right.

I'm an expert on textiles for the Local. I read up on the new materials like, so when management decides to fix up our image again, they will give us the real goods. Style and stuff that will make us feel snazzy all day.

Uniforms are a problem. The letter carriers going up and down steps and holding the addresses of the envelopes up to their faces to read them takes its toll on knees and elbows. It's an occupational hazard for the uniform, never mind their health. They're outside, walking about, that's their problem; ours is we're inside, under artificial light. Colours don't look the same inside as they do out. You can take a blood red out of the daylight and put it inside a mail station and it looks like veal. I gotta figure out what makes us look good and feel good so we're more efficient, without we work any harder.

I tell you, federal prisons got better décor than our mail stations at Canada Post, but it all boils down to being indoors. We end up as washed-out and grey as chickens that have bin lyin' in a pot of water too long.

Every year I give up on Hull and ever finding the cloth and colour that's going to make me look alive. Only one thing for it. I come down to Acapulco and turn on the rays.

Every morning when I take a look at her again, I think, maybe I got it wrong. Is it her or the bikinis are well made? They're super soft and glossy. Super fit. Like made-to-measure, but not the boyfriend – Gonzo. He doesn't fit her at all. A big bugger, like those wrestlers in the WWE must be before they go to fat and slob all over TV. Every morning she organizes the sunblocks, paints his nose and shoulders by numbers before she does herself.

As soon as she unties the strings of her bikini-top to lie on her front, she cups her breasts in her hands and twists round to see where he is. The way she leads him about! But I'd take to her leash like a dog, anyway. You bet, but I'm not hardly big enough to cross her notice.

Still, being big looks to this babe like more helpless. Like a guy's liable to bump into things, do himself damage. And the only part about me that's got bigger since I saw her wouldn't impress her none.

For a while, like, I believed the big lunk was a reetard – impaired, isn't that what we gotta say, or someways challenged? They tell us to at Canada Post. Now, her way of talking to Gonzo doesn't make him appear too swift. Her "*Bien, tu es content, maintenant*?" come out like he's been to the potty and is still in training. I suppose what she says shows she's real considerate of him.

You know I live in Hull, like, and work for Canada Post, so I've got the French Canadian and can tune in to these two, easy.

She's real chic. That short black hair. Chic, right – like women used to say when I was a kid? And her hands move like a hairdresser's over his head and chest.

Disgusting ash blond, silvery…real hairy chest. She ruffles it like you would a kid's. The hair on his head, and tits.

Tell you straight, I only fancy *her*, but it's the two of them I watch. The guy came second in the Handsomest Man of the Morning Show our entertainment girl put on at the pool. All the guys got paid a Piña Colada for taking part, and the top three got two. Ms. Bikini takes the second Piña Colada off him and sucks it, like it was some part of his anatomy she had oiled, personally, that morning

The latest: Gonzo's in a water polo game. Team captain. The entertainment girl Piña Colada's me into it too. "I guarantee you *all* get one for playing," says entertainment chief with the cute ass.

Trouble: the real entertainment – Best Bikini in Acapulco – is behind the goal, which is made up of these red traffic markers that look like hose-ends, or nipples some guy ripped off of King Kong. Bikini gives Gonzo his what-to-do's for the game and takes photos of his ugly mug while I stand in the shallow end trying to fire one that'll score, but not hit her.

The other guys on our squad got their eyes down her cleavage and forget what to do with their hands. There's one, he's a basketball star on his school team, who's worst.

Keeps lobbing it up so she does a stand-up stretch and kneel-down to put the ball into the goalie's hands.

Our goalie complains about getting hit by the ball 'cause it's too soft and keeps skipping off the water and into his face. He's blattered and blinded, he says, and every time the big guy's arms come down, they spray water in our goalie's eyes. Our goalie just wants Gonzo to let him get on with eyeballing her.

The big lunk scores six or seven times and does a smile for the camera, so when I go for the ball, I decide that I'll forget to stop my fist. So, while the big silver-grey gorilla plucks the soft green rubber ball out of the water like a lump of snot, there's a crack. His nose is gone for sure, I tell myself, but the hair on his pectorals just chokes me as he rolls away on his back and takes me with him on top of his chest and belly. I flap on him, like he's an oil drum. I hit him alright, but on the skull. Which he kept bent forward, chin tucked into his throat.

His eyebrows pucker and bristle with bubbles.

But give Bikini her due, she lays into the bugger for nearly drowning me. "*Gonzague*," she yells, "*ce jeux n'est past serieux. Aide lui la, pêche vite pour le pauvre petit poisson.*"

You know how Quebeckers say pêche, like it's pish. "Pish yourself," I splutter. Gonzo's big forearm is over my shoulder, his hand under my chin, trailing my head off my body toward the wall while he leaves the rest of me behind to drown.

As soon as he throws me at her feet, and as soon as she finds out I'm from Hull, Quebec, she wants to know all about my flight, what I paid, and what I do for a living. Gonzo, the wrestler or a buffalo-butt football player, says damn all and leaves the grilling to Cecile. That's her name, Cecile Gendron. Wife of Gonzague Gendron, the ape.

Once she hears I work for Canada Post, she laughs and says, "You guys are the weightlifters." Gonzague makes a fist and moves it up and down, like he's supposed to be holding a post bag. Except, I see it like a dead chicken whose neck he's just wrung.

I say, "A letter carrier's got a limit to what they carry, CUP-W won't let us inside workers touch bags over 20 kilo."

Now, a conversation on labour rules and regulations takes place.

Gonzague gives me his top-dollar advice. "Carry more. Good practice, that," he says and he winks. "Good for muscles, good for business."

"I'm not in the business of muscles," I tell him and he laughs, slaps my back so hard he leaves fingerprints on my shoulder.

Good for business. I smell a gorilla for the Chamber of Commerce and I hit confrontation mode: "Bags go out, bulging with flyers. Get me? 'Cause they're flyers, the guys in business think they're flying light as air. Ask a paper maker, he'll tell you a ton of paper is a ton, no matter what feather-brained guff's printed on it."

I'm waiting for his fist to send my head on a holiday, but he laughs and says, "Canada is not the Canada without the Canada Post and Monsieur Parrault at the CUP-W."

Anyway, we are on speaking terms, and Cecile always makes sure to bonjour me and ask again about how best to mail her postcards – in an envelope, or just the bare card... "Which?"

I say. "Letter-carriers and CUP-W people need to see somethin' sunny in the winter, it puts pizzazz in their day to see where you are. Think of poor stiffs doing miles in the snow and then they get a view of Aqua-puko." Aqua-puko goes right over her head. "Don't hide your fun in an envelope, it won't arrive any faster – just lick the stamp."

The big guy just shakes his head and looks me in the face like we all got a permanent hole in our satchels at the Letter Carrier's U and CUP-W.

It's Saturday, and the speedboats are dragging the parachute riders round Aka-puko bay. Like kids flying their own dumb fucking kites. What am I mad at? Mexico City has emptied its sewers and the shit has finally reached Aka-puko for Christmas. The joint is jumping with crowds of high-class and low-class Mexicans – nobody told me all kinds of Mexicans got the money to make it to Acapulco.

Now, on the pool deck, there's major movement. That lambada, man, like having stand-up sex in a roller coaster. No contest I want a part of, but the big guy and Cecile got it right. Finish your tanning at the pool by eight-thirty, then hit the beach and leave the young Mexicans the lumbago.

I make sure to watch Gonzague and Cecile take their first dip of the day in the ocean. Him on his back, Cecile on top. She paddles into the waves, her chin tucked into his tits, paddling him, her buns bumping up and down, her legs and bare parts of her body floating like brown silk over the top of him.

Now Gonzague decides to up, up and away on a parachute tow. Cecile's mad at him because he took off when she fell asleep and the lambada competition blasting out behind just won't quit because they've had hundreds of entries. Latin geriatrics are in, fakin' it with the samba. Two hours of heats for the lambada, and know what? I realize that Mexico City smog is just a cloud of brown B.O.

It's not that I'm prejudiced, there are just too many of them for me to put up with. I talk to Mexicans, say "Hi" and "*Buen aprovecho*," even ask them the age of their kids that go roaring around, and when I say there's no end to them, this one guy from D.F. – that's Mexico City – informs me, "Ju Quebec people, we know ju peoples. Ju think ju have the problems becoas the rest of the Canada doan like ju. Ju know they got bumper sticker say HAGA ALGO PATRIÓ-TICO, MÁTATE UN CHILANGO – Do patriotic thing, kill a chilango." I ask, like, are these Chilangos some vermin? "*Correcto*, we the vermins from Mexico City. We Chilangos for we eat very much chile."

Anyways, I tell the Mexican, I'm on holiday from all that Quebec and Canada problem, and he tells me he's on holiday too, from their Mexico City problem.

Too much! There's the big guy going by again already, waving at Cecile from his jolly jumper in the sky. He's easier to see up there than most, and after a while he's heading in for his landing when there's this jerk. Some gust of wind – or the seams in the chute give and down he goes like a gannet. One of those dive-bomber birds, trailing the red chute like his blood and guts behind him.

While he's been up there, I bin down here, nodding at Cecile, making signs, pointing up at him, making like he's a big toy we can both enjoy. I'm getting it worked out how to tell the Chilango shit in French, maybe I'll get a laugh out of her. Maybe enlist some sympathy from a fellow Quebecker on the discrimination issue. We got committees and investigations on that in CUP-W. With Parrault you bet CUP-W workers got respect for Quebeckers. That guy'd wrestled a bear to get the membership a fur coat for the winter. Straight as a die even though he spat French and English out the side of his mouth, like both languages tasted terrible.

Anyway, Cecile's a Parrault type. Cutting like a knife for el Gonzo, ready to disembowel a Great White for him. Under she goes, then his head is on her shoulder, and she's dragging him and the parachute.

Mighta been his shroud if she hadn't gone down and got a hold of him, for the Mexican guys in the boat haven't got a grip on it. Their hands are all up in the air and by the time they put them in the right place, she's ashore.

Lays him up on the beach, parachute still dragged out behind him in the water, but she has to spend more time beating at the curious crowd than on Gonzo.

Finally, I'm into it. It's my scene – mob control in the strikes. I can turn 'em on, lead 'em away. I jump in and spread my arms over him like he's a bomb and I'm shielding the silly fuckers behind me from certain death. I move back, getting the old arms wider, taking these Chilangos with me, and sure as usual, they fall for it, they move back.

Cecile has her two fingers down Gonzague's throat to get his tongue out, then she blows at his hairy mouth, and pretty soon he barfs and sits up, bigger than ever. Cecile falls back on her butt beside him and Gonzague stares at me, with this mob of Mexicans leaning over behind me. His body must have washed up and left his brains behind for he asks me, not seeing right – like, "*Qui m'a sauvé?*" which sounds very much like Tonto's "*Quiemo sabe*" in the Lone Ranger. But when she nods at me, he hits the sand so hard with his fist, he buries his arm up to the elbow.

The crowd at the backs of my arms gasps – glad I saved them from a dose of knuckles. Me, I haven't uttered a word.

For four days after that, Gonzague Gendron doesn't say a word, just glares at my jugular in a way that makes my Adam's apple jump. "He's a gentleman," Cecile keeps telling me every day, "who always pays his debts."

"Pay? What for?"

She doesn't answer that one, just says Gonzague will take me out on the town, and she delivers him to my door, dressed up in his grey suit, white shirt and pale puke tie. She's in her wrap, telling him to look after me, even giving my blazer a tug.

So, I like blazers, I tell the Gendrons. You can wear them anywhere, any time of the year. It's got a CUP-W crest, which gives Gonzo a giggle. "The *Capitain* CUP-W," he starts, "we have the table at Los Hongos. My wife, Cecile, she make the reservation, an' over the telephon' she choose the menu for the man who save me." Cecile smiles and next off, puts us in a taxi at the Copacabana ramp. Then, we're away – silver gorilla and CUP-W.

He's polite and his English improves as he goes, my French gets all junked up. Turns out he's a partner in an advertising agency. Would have been a copywriter till the cows come home, he says, 'cept for Cecile. She's thirty-eight, he's forty. They have two kids still in school, staying with her parents in Montréal. The parents and them will be down later.

I'm forty-one and a bachelor. He's just the son of a farmer, did this degree in letters, too shy ever to say a word in his class. I'm noddin' and listenin', scared I'll make an ass out of myself about her when he talks about his Cecile. Gonzague reaches over and grips my shoulder.

"You save me?" he asks me, but it's a question I haven't the guts to answer. "How you feel? *Capitain* CUP-W save a farmer's boy, or a big business executive – which you prefer, *Capitain* CUP-W? I use to be real rough. Her family…" he kisses his fingertips, "*Cordon bleu.*"

The day's special is mushroom stuffed with shrimp on Witchey-nango… Witchey-nango, chiley-nango – I'm thinking the fish is a relative of Mexico City folks that somebody killed. So, I go for a portion of fresh tuna steak and *haricots verts.* I am going back over everything I eat because it might be coming up again. Gonzo's fingers are drumming away, agitated as hell, like he wants to play a Jerry Lee Lewis number on my throat.

"You save me?" he says this all over again.

This restaurant, Los Hongos, is real ritzy, but the patrons all look like prime rib and lobster eaters, if you get the picture. Plain sorts sitting down to fancy food on their holidays. Then, Gonzo raises his glass, sticks out his hand and hauls me up with him, points me at all the people in the place and he gives them a bit of his Spanish. None of them looks too pleased. A couple of guys have got up and for no round of applause either.

"What did you tell these people?" I ask.

"That you save me. You pick me up out of the sea with one hand and save my useless life. You are an Anglo and have balls twice the size of their brains, or their wallets."

"That's one good speech," I say. "You should have saved it for my gravestone."

"You are one tough guy, you save me from drowning and a fate worse than death."

"From what – the bad breath of all those Mexico City guys gawkin' at you on the beach?"

That's when I tell him I never saved him. I've only gone along with it because she's told me to.

"And why she do that?" says he. "So I not feel helpless and beholden to a woman who save him from drowning in a ditch already, back on the farm, in Kweebec."

But the bugger kisses me, laughs and talks in Spanish, telling everybody in Los Hongos one more thing about me, one more for the road to hell I'm thinking. "I tell them I make mistake," he says. "You wish your brains and balls were half the size of theirs, and that you could spend the contents of your wallet on them."

For sure the bugger's in advertising. Work them up, work them down.

"I love her," he says, and his gush gets more embarrassing and hurtful than his public speaking. "Without her I would be a farm boy or a copywriter all my grown life." Tears are in his eyes, and he's kissing my cheeks like I was her. "CUP-W," he says. "She made me talk good French." And as soon as that comes out, his English goes strange. "It is the Noel," he says. "It is not good for a man to say he is more lucky than little Jesus in his Madonna's arms. You know, CUP-W. This woman she is my saviour."

Well, did I join him in this bit of lovesick heresy? No way. I'm gonna stick to old reliable. It'll be CUP-W that saves me, and no French Canadian Madonna, no matter how well made she is, or her C-cup bikinis.

Or little black dress she's stands in behind the door after Gonzo hauls me up for "le nightcap." (Only nightcap I want pulls over my eyes when I hit the sack in Hull.)

But, Hi-Ho, Silver! It's up to the penthouse with Gonzague Gagnon. One floor higher and God'd be sharing a slug of champagne with us. That's what Cecile holds out for her heroes – two flutes full of it.

Boy, do I glug and gag on my four ounces of bubbly. The jump to the 18th floor left my throat and stomach stranded on the 2nd, then, this roasting on Cecile's toast. "To our saviour…" Fine, since it's Christmas, right? Next, like the blast of a Mack truck's brakes, she lets out an oath, "*Sacre bleu, ça c'est sacrilèges!* Ah…" she looks at me… "*Le mot juste en Anglais? Oui,* our life saver!" I know 'n'uf French to yell, '*Moi, j'ai besoin d'un salvateur!*' But do I – no, though I bin burnin' at the stake all night for bein' a fake, and I'm wobble-headed, watchin' him winkin' and her drinkin'; then him drinkin' and her winkin'. The our-secret stuff between me and Cecile taps all the pep out of me, keepin' my trap shut, never mind the Gonzo and Cecile lovey-dovies. In front of yours truly, who's never seen a love letter cross the flap of his mailbox. I tell you that hole in my hall got so bad, I held other folks' hearts and flowers mail up to those big lights in cages that hang over the sorting-room. Love gush inside read as faint as my hopes of gettin' any love myself. Penthouse balcony scene with Gonzo and Cecile don't help either – all view and no prospect of me sharin' in the kissin'. Still, grace under pressure, that's me. I steal a line from "The Lady Is a Tramp" for my get-away. "Oh, what a night, such a beautiful night," says I, "but I bettah call it a notte."

Moon up there's on high beam for Gonzo and his girl. On the big dimmer for me.

I give my blazer a tug, salute, and leave them to it.

Sisters in Spades

Sister Felicitas scolds me. Usually, it is my bad calculus or lab book that gets it; this time, it's taking a spade from where it leans against what was the gardener's lodge, but which now serves as the school chemistry lab. The men who do the garden don't live-in anymore.

I can't believe Sister Felicitas took the spade from me so daintily. Outdoors, the gym-and-chem teacher grabs everything like a bat, but inside she is otherwise. This is the inside Sister, who handles the spade as she does tetrameters, beakers and slender vials to be stored in the lab fridges.

After resting the spade back against the wall, Sister Felicitas brushes her grey cardigan and pleated grey skirt.

"But why does he leave it here?" I ask.

"Who's he?"

"The gardener."

"Have you been watching one of the labourers… Have you some arrangement attached to this spade?"

The wood on the grip has a leathery glaze from the hands that use it.

"Sister Felicitas, would I ask *you* why the gardener leaves it here, if *I* had anything to do with him?"

I pose the point, logically, like the nuns teach us to. I get no answer.

"Should it not be away in the tool shed – out of the weather?" I wallow in saying weather, the Irish way, meaning rain.

"I caught sight of him," I say, choosing my words. "He wears leggings made out of old sacks, tied round his shins." Like a poor man's puttees, I think, but don't say.

"You are…if I remember rightly…a Waterston?"

All St. Ursa's girls are addressed by surnames, but I'm stumped at once by her "a," which puts me in my place through the Waterston collective.

"You know fine well I am, Sister Felicitas."

"And sent back."

I think Sister Felicitas refers to placement, my being put back a year into Fifth Form when I came from Mississauga to St. Ursa's in Ireland.

"What's your meaning, Sister?"

"Sent back to your old home," Sister Felicitas frowns. "The Waterstons are not supposed to touch anything to do with the property. Keep in touch, and your family has, but the property is to be left alone. Everything in the garden has its place, and it's not for you to choose where they go any more. How did you happen to see this…gardener?"

I point up to the window that looks down from our attic dorm.

"From our room."

"Then, you must be moved. We can't have our girls watching young men going about their work. Especially, a Waterston."

Once again, my curse of being a Waterston in the town of Waterston, in what was Waterston Hall. As bad as being the head teacher's daughter. Extra severity seeps into the Sisters' voices when they mention any deficit in my studies or appearance. Like some form of fat, I feel debilitated by Waterston money. My father did tell me to dig into my schoolwork, not our history. But said as if Dad insinuated I should.

In bed I often do a rewind mind-run on the toboggan down the slope from the back of our Mississauga house to the Credit River. In Mississauga, Ontario, I fill the slope with school friends to crowd out whatever my father, grand-mother and great-grandmother stare at there, on the slope from our house down to the Credit River.

I have had this luxury of Waterston women to advise and the family business to prepare me. Rosheen Waterston, my great-grandmother, filed the first records and searched for guests at the Toronto hub. The Waterstons have always run Lineage Hotels, which operate not unlike the Mormon Center in Salt Lake City with its worldwide family informa-tion and database. This feature keeps Waterston Hotels run-ning as continuous conference and research centres. But my father still speaks to my grandmothers and my mother about me as if I'm not there – even before I'm not there.

"Can she bear to be on her own with only memories of us to keep her company?"

"Memories are a man's distraction, but woman's daily bread. In any case, it's our trade," my grandmother harrumphs at him, and my mother won't even look up at my father from the chair where she sits, reading *Chatelaine*.

I quote her. "She abhors his absurd mix of sentimentality and trepidation at his decision to return his daughter to the fold, but then she only married into the Waterstons."

They gather in the kitchen, like it's their debating chamber. Kessie, the cook, uses a wooden spoon, a pot or a pan like a gavel when discussion gets in the way of their eating or her cooking.

They settle my switching schools over a seafood sauce and pasta-draining session. "The Grey Nuns will take care of her."

"The Grey Nuns?" I ask.

"Charity begins at home, in our case, our old home," I am informed.

I learn Waterston Hall was a gift to the Grey Nuns in Ireland, and Waterston Hall is now St. Ursa's School, where the nuns shall pass the benefit of their wisdom and instruction on to me. Amen.

"Okay, I agree to a good Catholic education, and to live without a friend in the world." Neither relieved nor pleased, they peer at me like I am one of Kessie's pots and colanders she has struck with her wooden spoon.

In Mississauga I would be going into Grade 12 after the summer break; at St. Ursa's I'm in Fifth Form. Put back and prickly as a pincushion about it, I badger to Sister Felicitas in chemistry over my top mark for my lab book. "Shows I should be in the Sixth Form," I tell her.

"Don't feel that you are behind, Jean. The Irish are always ahead of themselves in their educational standards because of their reputation for being backward, but then, the Irish always see their way forward by looking back."

"Sounds like everything slips into reverse, here! Even common sense," I say before I can stop myself.

"You are only going back a year, one of the hundreds."

From Waterston, a view of the Boyne lies in the distance. The lawned slope from the school leads into squared fields, clusters of trees and towns, a misty grid and something else of mystery and muddle haunts my heritage: this spade.

"Well, it's back for him when he comes to get it, later."

I startle Sister Felicitas with this reply.

"How much later?" she snaps.

If the young man props the spade opposite the girl's dorm, he does so for attention, but I don't disclose that I wait at the dorm window till he picks up his spade and takes it into the dark with him. Like a gaffer I keep a time sheet in an exercise book for him: his hours of departure and return. After a night's labour, shaking with exertion and steaming with sweat or dew, he leans on his spade, wraps his fist around the handle, which digs in under his breastbone, like it's giving him a paralyzing punch to the pelvis.

When I gently open the window, I hear the same thing every night: "'Taint no way enuf. Nine hours solid, and bad as ever, when I've done. Not'in' where it shud be."

This last night, before the Sisters move me, I'm down beside him, exercise book and pen in hand, to ask a question.

"Where should everything be?"

"Where it was."

I flinch at this and wonder if he has seen me touch the spade.

"Trenches were easier, Miss." He wipes his hands on his hips. "You're not angry at me, are you?" he asks.

"Should I be?"

"Perhaps not – leastways, y'r' talkin' to me. Nobody else is. Disgusted, are they?"

"I think it best I don't speak for the rest."

"Well, I put in the hours, Miss. Thousands and I'm beat."

"But you haven't given me your name for my records!"

I never knew I could sound so bossy and bold.

"Bowse Cartey. Do you not remember – the only one who volunteered?"

Now, he stalks off on me, giving me the view of his back.

"Volunteered for what?" I call after him.

A letter to my dad gets one from my grandmother back: "*Bowse Cartey joined Sean Redmond's Southern Volunteers in the Great War. He planted perennials, torch lilies, to come back to, and never saw them. Over there in Belgium, mortally wounded, a Grey Nun nursed him on his deathbed, and in a delirium, he proposed to the nun. People on the estate said he might have confused the nun with Cissy Waterston, who would be your great-great-aunt, were she alive. Bowse followed Cissy with his spade held across his shoulder, like a rifle, as if he were honour guard for her special projects to brighten the gardens. The photo of Cissy will let you understand the added confusions for Bowse with you.*

I can see.

Cissy's me with a lovely ruffle collar, running around her neck and all the way down to her waist, *small as a wasp's*, like my grandmother says. *Not Cissy's choice for the photograph, but done to please* her *grandmother. As for the nun, at eighty years of age she finally came over with her order to our gift of Waterston Hall and with this wish from Cartey: for her to visit him where things would look their best.*

They all shook hands at the handing over to become St. Ursa's. My father always said the nun wore a smile when she looked past them all at the garden, and she talked to it, "Tu sembles bien, mais pas heureux – fatigué, comme tous les homme qui travail pour rendre la nature de plus en plus belle dans son lit. Tu est fiel plus longtemps que la mort."

That was the last look she took at anything in this world. Funny old nun, she had been one of the negotiators, responsible for relocating the order after the War.

Which war?

This much leaves me feeling like the Belgian nun: a little light in one hemisphere. *We know whatever is up with him, you will put him straight. You're a Waterston and you're a woman* – end of Granny's letter.

When did I have my family graduation to woman?

Several days after I'm moved, Sister Felicitas says my eyes look unhealthy. They have shadows under them like I boot-polished them to pull on a helmet and play some ridiculous sport. Or go on a night raid.

Will I or won't I tell her?

To my mind the sister is SF. Her initials, and being into science and gymnastics makes Sister Felicitas as fantastic to me as science fiction. If she's not in the lab, she's in the gym or on a court coaching. Maybe Cartey comes to moon over her. Half of the girls do, some in the demurest and some in the dirtiest way, choosing to work out on the exercise benches or the courts till their nipples stick through the blots of sweat on their sports halters and their armpit hair is treated like *the* badge of bravery.

"Has he said anything to you?" Sister Felicitas asks me.

I don't know what to answer, so I quote him: "'I can't get it right. The place is as bad as ever.' I think that's it, but he mumbles."

"Is that all?"

"No, he said I'm a Waterston. Miss Waterston, actually, and it's all right for me if I keep track of him."

"For you to what?"

"Keep track. Until you moved me, I kept a time sheet of all the times he came and went with his spade in an exercise book."

"Is that so? And he talks like someone who isn't trying to get off with you?"

"Sister Felicitas. He talks like he's an employee and I'm his supervisor."

"Mistress would be a better word. Well, you'll have to give him his marching orders, eventually."

"I will?"

"You're a Waterston, as he said."

I'm flabbergasted as Sister Felicitas kisses my cheek.

"Time to get these fixed," she says to the bags under my eyes.

Since so many of the pupils at St. Ursa's have parents in business, Small Business Essentials is on the curriculum for the upper-level girls. We don't ever ask, "What about big business?" One girl who did was told, "For big, do the same, only more."

Taking on and laying off, humanely, is introduced, since many of us – the privileged – will be called upon to do it, and therefore are fit subjects for the topic. Once upon a time, we are told, dismissal training would have been for suitors, a specialty of the finishing schools, but the sisters are here to prevent us from cutting people dead and conducting an inhumane and spiritless business.

"For most," Sister Bénédicité tells us, "the hardest lesson is learning when to quit. In an ideal world we would recognize our own incompetence or redundancy. We should see it in our own faces, but that isn't the way it works."

I have the creepy feeling I am the sole object of these weird remarks or someone sitting directly behind me is.

During history, Sister Beatrix reprises the insult to Redmond and the Southern Volunteers. No officers, unable to issue their own orders. They stood in wait for commands to be given by Englishmen, which suited some.

Is that what Cartey waits for?

I see him at the end of the nine-hour night, leaning his head against the chemistry lab wall. He twists his fist on the handle of his spade, like a throttle. He mutters at me or someone, doubles over till the top of his head buries itself in the ivy on the wall. He reaches down and plucks at the sacking around his trouser bottoms, like he's trying to read the few letters that are left there from the brand of sugar it held.

"Well?" he says, and turns to look at my exercise book and pen, then my wristwatch. I tap my pen on my exercise book.

"Just say the word."

"You're sacked," I say, experimentally. Then, without a second thought, "Pick up your things and go."

His relief frightens me. It's like lightning.

As for Bowse Cartey's work and enslavement to loyalty, I'd love to find a torch lily he planted, especially when I discover it's a nice name for a red-hot poker, and take it in to Sister Cecilia, who teaches botany and music. But I come across no such thing. The gardens are all low-maintenance. Perhaps it's better so, otherwise Bowse might come back and spend eternity seeing to the torch lilies' welfare.

LILY OF THE BELLY

Lily's début engagement was at the Candia Taverna on 10th Avenue. Initially, the Candia suggested vouchers and Herbie said okay. The Taverna did a good pizza, great chicken and Greek salad. Herbie liked the wooden booths – maybe stalls described them better – for four or for two people. One served a party of twelve by the window; the cops used it, which added an aspect of public safety to the cuisine.

This double-sided row of dining stalls ran from the front door down to the bar at the back. To Lily, her Candia Taverna performance – swinging her hips, raising her arms, clicking her fingers and looking down at the diners, who looked up at her from their fodder in the stalls – was like belly dancing in a stable. Too much wagging in the aisle and Lily's lace skirt would be soaked in sauce, but the cash was easily stuffed into Lily's belt as she passed. Even the city police came back and poked in the odd five spot for her seven o'clock show.

People would be dipping into their *fasolada* soup when Lily's brown belly appeared right beside the pale brown beans. Doh-ray-me-fah-soh-lah-doh soup, Herbie called it because a while after you supped it, the stuff sang.

The next venue was the Achilles on Broadway. Here Lily had a centre to the floor, but it wasn't as good as the Candia for getting her belly into close quarters with the customers. However, the ambience of whitewashed walls, hinting at poverty and parched afternoons by the Aegean, turned the hunger and thirst on. Wine flowed between its larger selection of tables, and with those in the balcony upstairs, its numbers made the belly business there more lucrative than at the Candia.

While Lily danced, there was always a pause while the guys got over their embarrassment and pegged a bill to her belt. It happened as soon as they saw the women were more enthusiastic about Lily than they were. For Lily always danced to the women, demonstrating what women of her age had, what they could do with their own belly, if they had a mind to.

Herbie spent a lot of brain power explaining it to himself because he was both jealous and excited, no matter how hard he tried to keep business-like about it and just count their assets: his favourite, the kidney-shaped tub and Jacuzzi, added on the strength of her gyrations. Sometimes Lily would turn the jets off and agitate the water herself, for the exercise and to give Herbie a thrill. Lily, the one-woman whirlpool.

But her waters never broke in the way a woman's should. Maybe Herbie was too comfy with her at home, too sedentary, driving and delivering, waiting while his balls got grilled in the winter with the car heater on, waiting till she whipped through the back door and out into the alley in her trench coat.

So many stops at Greek Tavernas along Broadway and up 10th Avenue. Herbie wondered if there was enough feta cheese left in Greece for the Greeks to eat.

He watched them wheel the stuff in by the barrel along with the olives. If he ever did poke his nose in the back door to see her show, he caught the pails of Kalamata stench from the olives! Those times, the cooks would pass Herbie samples and before long his cholesterol was two times what it should be and he would sit in their kidney-shaped tub with his own testimonial to the belly sticking out.

Lily said she liked him fatter, and now that he was, she told him they could do some belly ballet, but Herbie wasn't so sure she wasn't screwing herself in the mirror of his belly.

As for Herbie not being able to make her a kid, it left him feeling condemned to be her bouncing babe in the bath.

One night there was a knock-knock at his car window in the lane behind Achilles.

"Business good?"

There was this new officer, fresh out of the Justice Institute on 4th Avenue. He pointed at a set of wooden steps going up to the flat-topped apartment over the store, next to the Achilles.

"Girls have been running in and out of there, pretty steady."

"Those are the Chou girls," said Herbie.

"Uh-huh, and who would the Chous be?"

"The girls you see downstairs in Chou's fruit and veg – Broadway Greens is what they call it."

"Uh-huh," the constable nodded. "I got a few girls myself. Makes you worry. What about you?"

"No girls, no boys. That's why Lily, the wife, took up belly dancing. Lily of the Belly is her trade name."

"Nice and catchy."

"We think so."

"And you wait to see if she gets out safely?"

"I do."

"Sensible of you, sir. Traffic down these back lanes isn't all blackberry pickers."

"Uh-huh, here she comes."

The constable straightened up to look over the top of the car at Lily. He blinked at the beauty spot and the stars she had sprinkled on her body to give it some flash when she danced.

"We were talking about the Chou girls and the officer's daughters," Herbie informed her through the window.

Lily nodded to the constable and gave Herbie a look as she swung herself and the trench coat she had tightened around her into the car.

Herbie immediately started the car and looked at the policeman through the open window, taking a moment for a polite farewell, when the uniform introduced himself as Constable Cone.

"Some men," Constable Cone explained, "have a little message in them that says: make women…" And before he had the chance, most likely to add, 'It would be nice to have a boy,' Lily leaned across Herbie to ask him, "Which way do you mean make and how many have you made?"

"Three."

So, if he didn't say it, Herbie said it for him.

"And you're after a boy now, to keep you company?"

"Not really. I like that I've made women."

"You have…" Lily paused, "with a little bit of help from a wife, I hope."

It was dark and the rain started. A drop or two bounced onto Herbie off the peak of the constable's cap. Lily had settled into her seat with the trench coat still wrapped tight, but her knees poked out as brown as Kalamata olives.

She kept up her colour at the Tanning Parlour on Dunbar, climbed into that coffin with those lights once a week. Part of the overhead, and white flesh frightened Lily.

In the dark of the car, the constable couldn't see what colour her knees were but with the proximity of the cop, Herbie could almost taste them in his mouth.

Home, and in the house, Lily laughed at him, "What are you licking at those for? You should have gone into the kitchen at Achilles. They would have looked after you."

"I'm off Greek food," said Herbie.

"You are," and she looked down at his head between her knees. "Don't go skinny on me," she warned him.

He lifted his head from Lily's round, deep brown thighs. In the mauve light cast by the lampshade above their bed-side table, her skin turned the colour of eggplant, and it put Herbie in mind of a Chou girl, standing with one in her hand, badgering her father about a boy.

She wanted to bring this boy home. Every time she whispered the boy's name, she lifted the eggplant closer to her father's face.

"You always waan a son, doan you?"

Old Chou took the eggplant from her and walked over to the place for the eggplants, patted it and gently set it down.

"That belong to some guy who pay good money. Egg-plan not your doll. You waan play house with this boy? You know he jus' waan come eat off us – he jus' a refugee from Mainland. He migh' be communis' spy, aan still think what udder people got is his."

Herbie bought that eggplant. He brought it home and watched Lily cut it up and batter it for the pan. He kissed both Lily's knees after that lovely dinner, on the tops where they were sticking up out of the tub.

"You like eggplant?" Herbie asked, gazing at the deep brown, almost purple glaze on Lily's knees in the bath, a long while after that episode with the Chou girl and the egg-plant. "You like it, don't you?"

"Herbie, are you all right?" Lily scoured Herbie's face for an answer.

Herbie realized Constable Cone kept up a casual surveillance on them. It broke up Herbie's Friday or Saturday night if he came by to talk.

At Achilles or the Candia, he'd stand beside Herbie's car out back, as they waited for Lily. Herbie joked Constable Cone about waiting there to arrest the berry-pickers in the back lane, if it was blackberry time. At other times he'd say to him, "Still here, trying to get a hold of those squatters…" – a family of skunks that had burrowed under a telegraph pole in the lane behind Achilles and arranged their lodgings underground in such a way that the pole began to tilt.

"Haven't I told you, Herbie, I'll leave the skunks to B.C. Hydro," Constable Cone would answer on cue and chuckle.

Then, one time Herbie asked, "You're not hanging out here to see if the Achilles is seasoning the salad with hash instead of oregano?" – but got no answer.

"It wouldn't be right to evict them," Constable Cone changed the subject.

Herbie wasn't sure if Cone was referring to the Chous because Cone was looking up at the railing on the Chous back deck above the storehouse.

"I saw them go in. There's three of them."

"Three?"

Then, Herbie realized Cone wasn't referring to the Chou girls, but to the skunks. Herbie asked Constable Cone if he wondered why this skunk family never sprayed or caused a nuisance.

"Maybe because it's too near home and they don't want to draw attention to it."

"Or they're out all night doing their rounds," Herbie added his two bits.

In any case, neither Cone nor Herbie ever caught a whiff of that burnt-out rubber smell, as Herbie described it, or the underarm odour of a thousand-year-old armpit, as Lily once told him, being very body-conscious at the time, after a performance and getting into the car, lifting her elbow and wrinkling up her nose, like she inhaled an exact match.

Herbie was telling Cone about this and they were laughing, when suddenly the lights over the back door to Achilles died like a pair of eyes and Cone quick-marched for the door to go see inside what was up. Ten minutes later, the lights came back on and Cone appeared with his arm around Lily.

Somebody had thrown the main breaker inside, and somebody else plucked the money off Lily's belt while trying to feel her up, and poor Lily was still dancing as hard as she could on the spot, there, in the dark. She began to wallop anybody who came within range of her hands. Tramped the tiled floor and shook faster and faster in a tantrum, her belt and tiny clappers jangling, like a hundred little cymbal players in a mad Salvation Army Band – or a whole set of alarm bells.

One of those who got hit was Cone, approaching her to offer assistance. But that wasn't the worst. In the car, Lily told Herbie how Cone said it would be awful for anybody to maul her. Like somebody pawing over his mother.

"What did you say to that, Lily?"

"I told him. 'What would you make of a mother, belly dancing, who never had a baby?'"

Cone was back inside to check if there was someone with Lily's scratches on their face, for they would be the robber. Basic detective work. Lily had told Cone she did get her claws into the bugger, but not deep enough. Then, in the dark – who knows? It may have been that the bastard was putting money in, not taking it out. She kept dancing on the spot, waiting for the candles to be lit. Damn odd they hadn't been, on every table, from early on.

Was Lily just a distraction, and Cone went into the Achilles, snooping after something – a kafuffle over something gone wrong? A knifing, under one of the tables. A few sharp knives had found their way into legs, other than legs of lamb, lately. Goons liked Greek food, too. And drug pushers.

After his mother remark that went wrong, Cone invited Herb and Lily to see his little girls. Lily made such a fuss over them, it was natural for them to treat her like a grandmother. But Herbie said nothing. The appeal of getting to be a grandmother without ever having had a kid of her own wouldn't last long for Lily. It was inevitable. She looked all mother, and now she was that touch older, a young grandmother.

The dancing took the edge off her years, a well-exercised belly ages well and doesn't let a woman down. Rolls of flesh can grow around a tummy like the rings of a tree, but given the right shake, jangle and roll...! Really and truly... Lily talked belly sometimes till she made Herbie sick. Her shtick about the belly had big words in the middle of it – omm, omphalos, ovum, centrum. When Lily got religious about it, you'd think the money was like what comes on the collection plate at church, a donation for life's oldest tabernacle.

If robbed her belly was in Achilles, for Lily it was sacrilege. Those godawful engineering students from UBC it had to be – the ones who stuck a poor girl on a horse every year and had her play Lady Godiva, buck-naked in February.

On the night, during their visit to his home, Cone told Lily and Herbie he had taken names and discovered this spot of what he called some other trouble.

Herbie went "Uh huh," and Cone asked if he could take Lily down to the Achilles in the daytime early, and to the station afterward. Lily's report on that sequence of investigation. When they were talking to the manager, she said she could scarcely sit in Achilles, the questions were all about these people Cone had on a list in his notebook. Were they all possible belly robbers or what?

"Uh-huh," said Herbie to Lily on that.

Herbie hadn't been privy to any of this. He had to take care of his day job in the body shop. Other than Nigel Cone's driving Lily to the Achilles and the Main Street Police Station in the daytime, Herbie didn't feel excluded or jealous. But come to think, Lily out there in the broad daylight, minus all her veils and bangles, was like seeing her naked. Herbie trusted Lily in a crowd of horny men, but alone with someone, without red lipstick, eyeliner and sparkle on her body – Lily's bare belly was public, her everyday face, not.

All this came to Herbie when she was reporting her investigations with Cone.

Then, Lily started reliving the fright for the fun of it, which relieved Herbie and made Cone none too happy.

She turned it into an excuse for being unpredictable and wild. If Herbie touched her unexpectedly, she would spin and slap at his hand.

Once, he accidentally nudged her with a plate of cheese and crackers from behind, when she was sitting watching television, and she swiped it across the room. She watched the soft inside of the Camembert stuck to the wall, while the creamy crust hung like a slice off of somebody's skin. Then, Lily ate it off the wallpaper, pressing her lips into the design as she did this.

As soon as she saw how startled Herbie was, she licked his face, like he was another piece of cheese she'd missed. Her tongue and the Camembert on the wall made him crawl, in a good and a bad way. Then, she turned the lights out at the switch.

"Did you like that new daytime driver of yours?" Herbie finally asked her his shy question.

"What Nigel showed me made me think," was her answer. "Those girls that dance down there in the pubs, where the police headquarters and the courts are on Main. They're as skinny as Nigel's little girls. Taller, of course, and right – even if they are all bones, you'd be amazed at the mad dogs who come slavering up and want to gnaw on them. Nigel said I should think twice about putting my sex on show. We just make his job harder."

Herbie knew by the look on Lily's face that this bugged her big. Nigel had shown her the cop shop, then the sex-show shop.

Herbie looked down as if reproaching his hands.

"Pity I'm not licensed to carry a gun," he said, "or I'd've put a hole in that smash-and-grabber."

"No reason for you to turn cop, or killer – Herbie. You'd be committing suicide."

"What?"

It was the evening of the Camembert on the living room wall.

"I know you thought, if you scared the hell out of me, Herbie, things would change."

What the fuck did that mean? Herbie was the guy at the breaker *and* at her belt?

As soon as she swept the lights out that night, she whispered in his ear, "There, that's how it feels to be grabbed in the dark."

Herbie groaned, looked around in the gloom as though all the customers' faces in Achilles were boggling at him.

The odds against his being in two places at once, in the car and hitting on her in Achilles, were the same as his being able to make her pregnant. Astronomical.

Even at the best of times their doctor said a man's semen was just like stars, or the white dots on the dice sailing through the dark womb of the universe. Their doctor also said he could try to arrange something, but Lily wanted no genetic engineering, no medical mixing and matching, or calendar-watching like they were a pair of fee-paying ancient Mayans.

Over a year after that, Herbie was dozing behind Achilles with no Cone droning in his ear, when he heard the sound of sirens. He looked out the car window into the back lane. The whole Chou family was at the back of their apartment, on that deck with railings around top of the Broadway Greens storehouse, celebrating something. Herbie watched one of the daughters spin distractedly around the conversation of her father and a young man, while both stood, locked in a serious talk. About eggplants, Herbie guessed.

Then, he saw the mother come out to announce dinner. She was waving her hands and trying to pull everybody inside, but the company on the deck all had their hands on the rail by now and were gazing out over the top of Herbie's car to where the wail of the sirens came from, down West Broadway, approaching from the east.

With a squealing of tires, a Buick cut into the lane, swept past Herbie's Chevy, only to find that the lane dead-ended by the Chous' truck, which old Chou parked ille-gally, to stop traffic using the back lane as a Saturday night short cut.

Immediately, the Buick went into reverse, the guys in the car geeked up at the Chous, even taking out a gun and mak-ing as if to fire to get rid of their nosiness off the deck.

The Chous grabbed the visitor in a howling frenzy, like he was the cause – the target for the wheel-spinning Buick and the gun in their lane.

At that very moment, Herbie saw Lily in the open back door of Achilles, trench coat on, ready to go. He had to get her out of any line of fire from those guns if those bozos met up with the cops in the lane. Shuffling across the front seat on his back, Herbie slid his passenger door open and as he did so he dropped one hand to the ground, ready to turn and use both hands to haul himself out and go protect Lily.

Bristles of stiff fur passed through his fingers. He caught a nose-ripping stench, as if the burning rubber of the get-away car and shit-scared fright of those in it had blown in around him.

The skunks had taken themselves out of the line of fire under his Chevy. Out of the car, panting, and over on all fours now, Herbie scuttled to see if he could get to Lily as fast as the skunk family got to its hole under the telegraph pole. If that was where they'd head – for home, like he did for Lily.

Herbie grabbed her by the double-breasted folds of her trench coat, just as the whirling red of the police siren shut off with an enormous thud behind them. The crash of it into the Buick busted the Buick's hood and bounced the Buick sideways into the scarred wood and dried creosote of the telegraph pole. The noise echoed until every piece of metal and glass had settled onto the lane.

Next moment the old pole was falling in the Chous direction, followed by a huge screaming and wailing in Cantonese and Mandarin. At the same time, a great fucking and blinding and "Don't move" orders came down the lane and into the back hall of the Achilles.

Herbie and Lily didn't budge till Constable Cone tapped Lily on the back and looked for Herbie, where they were both hunkered down and Lily had him pulled under her trench coat.

"You – and everyone else inside. Tell them to exit through the front of the restaurant. You don't want to stir-fry out back with the Chous," said Nigel Cone, and he didn't even grin.

All along, that was what Nigel Cone had come for at the Achilles. To scope one of the drug collection points. Herbie had read about it in *The Province* newspaper, the snoopiest of the two Vancouver rags. Shippers sent the junk, sunk in barrels of feta, Kalamata and the like – for which sniffer dogs were no use. Shipment details for the narcotics could be coded into a regular order. The heroin originating in Turkey or Afghanistan came into Canada via Greece – that whole place in parts of Turkey and up there Afghanistan being one big prairie and Alpine meadow full of poppies and poppy growers.

"The Chous are all trapped on their deck," said Constable Cone, swaying down the Achilles' back hall for a few steps with Herbie and Lily. Blood was starting to scribble down his face, running from under his cap, which he had put on, skewed, to cover the wound.

"You should have reported the skunks," Herbie told him.

Constable Cone had nothing to say. His face was still growing a fine mesh of blood

"Will you please go on in and tell the rest of them down there to leave the restaurant by the front door?" Cone repeated for Herbie as a cop, who must have been his partner, came up behind and caught him under the armpits before he fell.

When they looked down at where Nigel Cone might have smacked the floor, that's when they saw the skunk, by the size of it – a teenage kit, who'd followed Herbie and Lily. It must have hunkered behind them at the door, like Lily was its mummy, then moved into the Achilles under the tails of Lily's trench coat. So close on her heels, in fact, they didn't even notice. Cone was in no shape to take in anything much, but the instant Cone's partner's feet came sprinting down the hall, the kit let fly and clickety-clicked over the floor tiles and back outside

Out back, the pole had smashed into the Chous' deck, but not fallen completely. The broken lines whipped and sparked over the paintwork on Herbie's car. Heavier than ever, the stench of skunk compounded with the odour of barbecued paint. The entire skunk family must have let go another foul volley of warnings, exiting the opened ground and asphalt around the pole. The home they may have reached, only to be evicted and then meet up with their prodigal kit. The one that helped send Cone into a swoon.

Three men had been pushed into a back garden, away from Herbie's car and the cruiser. One, went through the glass into a hothouse, whose owner was outside, disputing the damage with a plainclothes officer.

The fire brigade was there now, and Nigel Cone, even as he was being helped out of the lane, calling to the Chous, who were no longer there, "Stay in the front, till we tell you the power's off."

As for the Chous, they had done as Cone said before he even said it.

The whole family had come out front onto Broadway with their young male visitor, or suitor, or whatever, along with the Achilles crowd to hear what was happening after the fireworks. Laughter started, and some crying. The crying indistinguishable from the Chou laughter.

"Our visitor say Chous a very together, very exciting family," old Chou shouted half-hysterically at Herbie and Lily, who had moved through and out of the Achilles, by then. Up Broadway in the direction of Broadway Greens.

As things relaxed, Lily's nose and Herbie's went into active operation again.

"Nobody'd have the guts to grope me in the dark now," said Lily.

It was true.

"Like Sonny used to say to Cher in Ringo's song, 'You and me, Babe,'" said Herbie, unable to divine if the skunking left Lily bursting with excitement or the desire to puke.

But what really must have done it to the sperm count was the tomato juice.

Ten of Libby's black and red cans of tomato juice. He enjoyed going through Safeway to get them. Everybody in the place watched him and backed away as he approached. He would come up one aisle looking for the familiar, tall, red and black cans, and that would push people up the aisle and round to the next, where the stench wasn't a tad easier. Herbie got into the rhythm of this, moving a small mob of shoppers from aisle to aisle. He was turning Safeway into a stinking maze; shoppers would have to find their way out of with their nose.

One of the junior shelf-stackers in his red waistcoat was yelling down at him, "What are you looking for?"

"Same thing as everybody else is looking for," Herbie shouted back. "Something to get the smell out."

"I don't know what would do that?"

"I do," shouted Herbie. "Tomato juice."

"Aisle 4. Middle."

They loaded the bath with the Libby's and got in. When he looked at Lily's skin with the tomato juice sliding over it, he said, "Your tits go with the tomato like mozzarella topping."

This was the first time in years he had said or seen Lily's tits. Of course, he had seen them, but didn't register how her nipples were as dark and oval as you know what, and against the happy-pap juice, the rippled umber, budding like stones out of the brown olives on the tops of her breasts, Lily's seemed ravenously white.

Everything gets started in such a stink.

They were ridiculous to look at and to listen to. They had an argument again over how to describe the smell. They made jokes about their car getting its battery recharged for free, but afterwards, in the wrecker's yard, they would touch the gashed paintwork with great reverence, where the lank end of one power line had twisted over the roof and hood.

Or perhaps what did it for Herbie was the fear, then after that, feeling safe inside her. Feeling scared and safe at the same time made him go, go and know where he was going. Yes, that was it. Being wide awake to her in the dark, going at it, not falling into the usual mope at not being able to take full advantage of all the work she put into her dancing for him.

$\mathcal{C}$L

Hell is full of the things people said they were just dying to do.
—HERBIE FERRIS

I am Gavin McFee. I have been given a commission by the BBC to track down and videotape my wife's school friends from the sixties, who have immigrated to North America from Northern Ireland. In this instance, the Corporation is my client; not so long ago, it used to be my employer, and now I supply features on a freelance basis to what we all used to call The Mother Corp. The specific contract is for my wife to interview and for me to serve as technical support and producer for the television programme. I see it as a personal and professional plus for me because I will be gathering her school friends' candid responses to Terry without having to put questions of my own, which could prove awkward or embarrassing.

Watching and listening to Terry disarm, then provoke her chums into revelations, is the natural order of things for me. I first bumped into her and her friends in their training-slips on the deck of the town's tidewater pool where they were gathered to represent their school in a relay.

My elbows came into contact with at least two sets of breasts and a shoulder as they shuffled to let me by. I was going to join my own school team and wait for the boys' relay which followed immediately after. I blushed wildly when one of the girls, El, took me by the hips to guide me by without further collision. Thereafter, I've never been able to encounter any member of Terry's set without the feeling that they never did put on their clothes (or a single year to their age), but now it is Terry who steers me between their bodies, as if they are indeed the same pneumatic girls I might jostle in my awkward middle age.

The town of B. is a seaside resort in Ulster, well known for its sterling character and beauty, and the girls at the Collegiate School are notorious for both. Some in my wife's class of '62 became women who wandered, which is the way with Ulsterwomen of a certain stripe.

Talent and discontent take them off, and it is in Vancouver, Canada, that we start to become reacquainted with a few of them and their reasons for leaving. Their own bafflement at why we have stayed through the "Troubles" and put up with the incessantly bad weather shows in their looks and flow of undisguised sympathy toward us. It is as though Terry and I had elected to remain on the deck at the pool long past the swimming season, our skin goose-pimpled by the bitter wind blowing off the lough.

The tidewater pool in B. has long since been closed, but is still traceable in the salty laughter of the Collegiate girls and their behaviour. They look at the overgenerous swell of

Terry's thigh under her skirt, the bulge of her breast. They touch each other continually with their eyes, holding each other and the memory of what they were with the palms of their hands while their conversation orbits around what they have done since then, which is a lot.

M. has flown up from Stanford, where she teaches after having worked twenty years in New York for the UN as an interpreter. J. is an MD married to a Church of Ireland clergyman, reclassified as Episcopalian when he landed in Canada. Let in, J. informs us, because Canada needed clergymen and their wives, not physicians – of which there were too many. J., however, practises at the CSTD (Clinic for Sexually Transmitted Diseases); another, B., is a trader at the VSE (Vancouver Stock Exchange, which has the sleazy reputation of a casino, but through its penny stocks – B. assures us – it promotes new mining ventures no one else would handle); and P., a former PE instructor, is now entrepreneur, proprietor of The Fitness Barn. My wife Terry, I should add, is a teacher in English as a Second Language, pursuing her second book in body language.

Terry notes that three out of four are into bodies and one is into money. They laugh with Terry at her observation, which, they agree, is true.

Bodies and money. Who is into both?

P. laughs and suggests herself and her fitness barn. Then, all of them talk instantaneously of El, in Nevada, and look down the lens of the camera, trying to see me. I am not sure how much of the footage that follows is usable. Since so much of it is gossip about El and with every glass of wine it grows more lewd and ghoulish; compassionate, then sentimental for the prodigal El. I already recognize these emotions may turn into a matter of dispute between Terry and myself in our room later.

Since it involves El, it is sure to. Terry has never told me Elizita is in America.

After pursuing the old girls of the Collegiate through their daily routines – J., at the CSTD; B., at the VSE – I am able to combine pictures of hands on the stockroom floor, brandishing buy-and-sell orders, with those of arms heaving a rhythmic forest of fingers in the air, which I shot through the windows of The Fitness Barn at eight in the morning. A fistful of images, as it were, of what gets the alumni of the girls' Collegiate up and going in Vancouver.

Money and muscle.

I take the thumping beat of music and feet of the early-morning exercisers to a clacking intermezzo of halyards and gulls on the masts of sailboats in the False Creek marina where P., the proprietor of The Fitness Barn, lives in a penthouse with her Swiss-Canadian husband.

On the last evening the conversation comes back again to El and her love life.

"She would die for it."

"She nearly did."

I can't work out which of the voices go with these two overly spontaneous remarks. Now, the consensus is that

Terry and I should go and do a story on El in Nevada. Does anyone have an address?

The physician, J., has a phone number. Elizita wrote to her once and gave her this in case of emergency. J. has provided Elizita with hers, for the same reason.

"What might that emergency be?" J. asked Elizita.

"A man, or your woman's things that doctors don't deal with, or the odd urge to visit Nevada," came the reply.

When they are serious on the matter of Elizita, the women admit that, except for her "odd urges," El did have common sense and was wise in the ways of the world, and *that* led her to try psychiatric nursing, which B. (the trader on the VSE) points out, drove her to put her head in the gas oven. Discussion erupts over state-controlled care versus support at home, which, because of responsibility to the family, obliges one to go out and find a job to supply the everyday needs, not to mention love. Somebody suggests that the intimate touch is what El truly understands.

"She's about as sensitive as a sea anemone," says Terry, draining her glass.

"Meaning?"

"Whatever floats by, whatever feels good, Elizita gloms onto."

J. looks at Terry, then at me; they are already holding on to each other's hands when J. speaks for both of them, "Let's phone and tell her you're coming." And before I can say Jack Robinson, J. is giggling into the receiver, "You're there, you're there. Lovely to hear you, El."

(Pause)

"No great alcoholic event. We're all here, just having a wee glass of wine with Terry and Gavin. You'll never guess what they're up to. Making a program on us Old Girls, so we thought – you've got to talk to Elizita."

(Pause)

"She wants to know who's going to talk to her. Terry or Gavin?"

"I'm not doing the interviews," I say, and Terry takes the receiver from J.

"That's fine," Terry shouts into the phone. "It's fine," she shouts back at us, moving at the same time and trailing the long cord from the phone to the table where J. is pointing to a pen and pad. "Wait a bit, wait." Terry begins writing.

"Can we all say something to her?" asks M.

"No, we've probably said too much already," says Terry. "She only wants to talk to me and she wants Gavin to come and video what she's up to."

Terry comes over, holding up a piece of paper for the camera on which she has printed: Clear Haven Hotel, McNair, Nevada. Night or morning of July 12. Phone: (702) 641-8899.

"Strange way to set up a meeting. Night or morning and the date, as though El's running an agency."

"Shows she's a professional, same as the rest of us," says B.

J. agrees, "Equal to any, or all."

"Even if she isn't," B. butts in, perhaps not feeling quite equal herself, "doctors aren't the only ones who can fix people up," she says.

"Are you going to fly or drive?" J. asks us in order to change the subject.

"Two days is enough for the drive, isn't it?" I ask.

"Then, you won't fly down with me," says M., who has already asked us to stay with her in Palo Alto so that she can show us Stanford.

"You'll still be there in a week..." Terry hesitates.

"And with El you're never sure where she'll be," M. agrees. "Alright, but you'll pay a penalty on your ticket for the change."

The repetitiousness of the fir forests in B.C., Washington and Oregon vanishes through the interior, where the coastal ranges and highlands turn into a plateau on the other side of the Rockies. The land appears to have been spread out to dry, like a great wrinkled sheet with dust the colour of blood blowing all over. It intimidates and infuriates me with a need for speed in the car. I drive in a daze of constant acceleration, as if the rising of the road will continue into an unrelenting sky that has magnetized the metal of the machine to its light. Something in me is geared to match its glare with velocity.

Could we cope with living here?

Our accents seldom fail to start a conversation wherever we stop. We become the centre of a warm huddle, setting fire to curiosity and confidences.

The good folk always explain who they are and ask where we are going; our lives and theirs are summed up in those few sentences we share along the way. One half of the life we have to tell about is our destination.

When asked, we answer, "The Amargosa Valley, to visit a friend, El., to make… Well, not really a whole programme, part of one that will have her in it for the BBC. She went to school with my wife."

One trucker who's driving a silver tanker of milk and wears a T-shirt that says

> *Got no Beef,*
> *All Pure Cow's Milk,*
> *no Bull*

agrees. *He* would do a programme on El. "Nobody better to do one on around the Amargosa."

"Why nobody better?" Terry wants to know, wondering – I'm sure, as I am – if this can be the very same Elizita, who is known by (what sounds like) her initial alone.

"Now don't go teasin' me, like you don't know," the trucker laughs at Terry from the door. "They must make you all like that over there. *Never tell in the daylight, what you do in the dark.*"

"What's that all about?" Terry asks me, as she is left listening to the truck driver sing a rougher version of what he has just said, outside,

> *"Never tell*
> *in the daylight*

> *the hell*
>
> *you fuck with all night."*

EL or hell? I am not sure what way we should hear the line.

Hour after hour of listening to the radio leads me to a morbid absorption in the lyrics of the songs, the miserable epitaphs and epigraphs about love, all manner of contrivances and conceits begin to appear genuine. Where does the *new* Country misery in the music come from? The *old*?

I wonder if I will use this song the trucker flung over his shoulder as the beginning of the segment on Elizita, or will I reject it? Odds are I shall veer away from the EL or the hell I might fuck with all night.

The way people talk here may sound rough and lazy, but there – in the steady, mournful tones they use to answer our question about how far we still have to drive – it drones as quotably as any lyrics on the radio: "Once your ass is bust, and your foot falls asleep on the juice, you've arrived, buddy."

It is the truth bottled in a hyperbole because I do ache after the driving.

Through the hill towns, the lyrics are runways of neon we drive into and out of – a line of song and spangle of light turning on and off like the radio. A bleak loneliness in them fits the endless break-ups we listen to in the ballads. The same feeling is mined as doggedly as metal in the mountains. And driving into the night, I feel I'm plunging into a mine – the roof, hung with lights, leading into deeper, gloomier shafts of darkness. Until I can see no end to it, no bottom to the achy-breaky heartland of prospectors and lonely miners, who dream of cathouses, or their wives smothering at home on the remoteness. One day they come up and their wives are gone, and all the men are left with are the songs.

I've been reading, I've been listening, preparing for this segment which will take place at the edge of Death Valley surrounded by ghost towns.

It is in the late twilit evening when we finally creep along the strip into McNair. The Clear Haven Hotel happens to be well over on the other side of town. Brick-built, in a residential area, less contoured in lights. Once more we have to drive into, then out of the town centre. In the lobby we stand, cooling our heels in fresh pastel carpet of a modern silver mine; we blink at the ranks of slot machines in the casino. Idly, we watch a man and a woman sit side by side, playing four at once; like a tag team of piano players, they keep the play buttons busy, picking up the heavy dollar coins of their winnings from the trays to feed back into the machine. Terry is reading a brochure she was handed at the door after the valet swirled away in our car.

DATELINE: *Adult Entertainment Guide & Forum.* Like the gills of a glossy fish, Terry splays the pages of the brochure for me. *Totally Nude, direct to your room.*

Page left has a brief account of the legal brothels of the Amargosa Valley; page right offers *The Sister Act:*

Cheryl and Marcy, who wear only origami stars on their nipples.

When we are shown up to our room, its pastel-restful colours don't lull us to sleep. I think of Cheryl and Marcy, angels gleaming in what the miners dream of above ground: one hell of a heaven. Terry and I argue about what I have shot during the day and we abuse the décor a while, trying to tire our minds out, but my eyes continue to look for the excitements that the darkness and the light of driving have accustomed them to.

Without telling me, Terry calls the front desk, to see if Elizita has checked in. No, she has not, but she's expected – as it says in the clerk's handwritten message from the front desk – tonight or in the morning. The clerk asks Terry if she wants to call El's number, or would she like a car to take us to her after we've unpacked. He can discreetly guarantee that El's is the best, the right choice for a visit – us being Europeans.

"Should we take a cab?" Terry asks, enjoying being able to say *cab*.

I shake my head. Her saying *cab* signals a change in her that I can't place.

Terry falls back on the bed, splaying her legs over the end, swinging them, then she throws herself up into shoulder-stand and her skirt falls down over her face.

Juvenilia, the sister act?

I go out of our room onto the balcony. The pool below us is longer than I expected – it might be a blue runway for one of the float planes, flying over here from Lake Tahoe. There are so many small planes, switching directions, turning into the hills, their lights moving along flight paths above and below each other.

Terry has come back to herself and is unpacking. She asks me only to look after the equipment – to hook up and play back the video on the TV. In the audio portion of the Vancouver footage, the Ulster accents thicken as the recorded conversations progress.

"Remember swimming round the American carrier in the bay? We were so cold, we could have taken our togs off and they would have thought we had blue swimsuits on."

"I would have screwed the whole crew, just to get warm," Terry turns deliberately to pronounce this for the camera.

"You would?" I hear myself come in obliquely from under the casing of the camera.

"What girl wouldn't?" they say in unison, standing behind Terry.

The planes lift and fall in air to the waves of voices. I close my eyes, leaving Terry to look at her friends on-screen.

I continue to dream in what I call my commentary mode. "There is a point in Pentecostal meetings," I am saying, "when people let everything go. With groups, this is the way. Two of the same persuasion meet in the street and you have a revivalist meeting, but opening your body to a congregation is hardly a religious experience, is it?" Then, I raise my hand in some form of testimony, and out loud I carefully count the seductions I know to have taken place on Methodist Church outings. The computation of purity and fornication in the one place dazes me.

The desert and the small morning wind appear to be made principally of light. At the same hour as the Collegiate girls used to climb over the wall to the outdoor pool, which was built at the bottom of the small cliff, under the school, at that hour. When I look down, there is Elizita, standing by the hotel pool.

"I told you she would be," Terry says so close to my ear that her lips touch it. The girls synchronized their sensuality young; it tied in with another near-mystical urge, being the first person of the day in the water. After that, the freshness of its blessing was gone.

The two of them, Terry and Elizita, walk toward each other and hug. The force behind their smiles begins to make their heads, then their bodies, shake. In the moments before touching, they adopt the walk of the hard men back home, as if they are approaching each other for a punch-up instead of an embrace. The hunch of the shoulders, the rough tongue they give to the greeting is several rungs in the vocal and social register beneath them. "How's about you, daughter?"

Elizita takes sight of me across Terry's shoulder. Her face sets.

I wonder if I should follow Terry with a hug, apply my lips to one or both cheeks. I choose a hug, and one.

"Elizita, you are…" She's waiting for me to pick a word. I go for one, "…what can I say, looking so, very…splendid."

"Jesus, Gavin. You're not still a grammar school boy, are you, talking to one of the governors' wives on Prize-Giving Day?"

She's given me my cue. "What the hell, El? You could be the prize. Life-size trophy, in that silver get-up."

"Never a truer word, Gavin. Never a truer word."

She glances at the camera case I have brought down with me and set on the glass tabletop, which gleams as brightly as the pool under it. She aims a moment without expression at the camera, then tells Terry, "He hasn't changed, has he? Still set to watch us girls to see what we're up to.

"Well, here I am, ready to be introduced to your viewers."

In her wrap of silvery silk and a pair of rubber pool shoes, I'm tempted to cap her quip about viewers with what pops out of Terry's mouth.

"Voyeurs, love."

"Oh, I luv it when you call me love."

I look down at Elizita's feet, at her pool slippers. They too are coloured silver. They make her feet look small, severed from the tan of her ankle and leg. Her hair is short. The silk and the chill of the early morning have braced her skin. It has a winter tan, like khaki, or like the skin of a potato that had been scrubbed and baked evenly and firmly in the oven. A smidgen of oil is all it will take to darken it.

"You look really great, yourself," Elizita says to Terry. "I bet you catch an eye or two that Gavin doesn't notice."

"Could be, but look at you," Terry replies. "Great robe – your whole outfit, great," and Elizita stares into my silence behind the camera. "Doesn't she just make you want to kiss her?" Terry says with a low, salacious hiss, like she's saying it into my ear.

"I already have, haven't I, Elizita, and I have chapped lips this early in the morning," I answer, trying to make them laugh and ignore me.

"What's 'e been up to that 'e needs Lypsyll?" Elizita asks.

"Putting his footage in his mouth," Terry says. "Come on and give Elizita a kiss."

"Doesn't matter one way or t'other," Elizita pouts in that North-of-England accent, which she brought with her to Northern Ireland, and has now imported to Nevada. "A touch of t'other does no harm though. Am I right or am I rat-shit?" she asks Terry.

"No harm," says Terry.

In B., Elizita was a touch of t'other from Birmingham, who joined the school at thirteen when her father was transferred to head the Inland Revenue division for Northern Ireland. In a short while, her class adopted her Birmingham way of saying things, especially *t'other*. T'other was touted everywhere.

"Remember the old pool first thing in the morning? Whatever was it Sandy put in it to keep us from getting the lurgy? Whitewash on the walls, chlorine…?"

"Fresh sea water and tea leaves," Terry continues for her. "Parts of the pool smelt like a cuppa with too much milk in it."

"Tea in the teeth. Remember when you got tea leaf in your teeth?"

"Remember those awful changing boxes that smelt of bums and armpits? Others used them for undressing, but not *we*. Sandy knew, y'know, that we compared our parts."

"Needed his cup of tea to keep awake in that equipment room. Well, one end of the changing boxes was the back of his equipment room, right? Had a slot in t' wall, for lettin' in air and coolin' the old bugger down. While us girls – out in the chill, tits standing to attention. Ready for inspection, right?"

Elizita gives the two fingers – which is one finger over here. Who to? The ghost of the old voyeur, or me?

"Gavin McFee, that man had his big peeper fixed on us, well before you came along with your camera. Now, let me look at you," she says, and I step back, thinking she's talking to me, but she tugs open Terry's gown that came supplied with the room, a whisper of silk which she found hanging in one of its closets – an entire gown comprising a Chinese or Japanese print of a bathhouse, where the women are on their knees beside the men in the porcelain tubs, washing them.

"As ready as ever," Elizita says to Terry, but looks at me and my camera, which I have taken out to set up on my shoulder, as if neither of us are there.

"My hump," I tell Elizita.

"A good hump never did anybody any harm," she answers. "Not so, Terry?"

While I fuss with the focus, Terry asks after El's ex, the one we know of. "How's Cecil?"

"Out of touch as usual," says Elizita. "You know Cecil. Thought it was his sensitivity turned me on, but it was t'other. After I opened the oven door in my dear old flat and woke up to tell the tale, I thought Cecil was the answer." She moves her head around, trying to see more of my face. "Near-death experience makes a girl horny. I suppose any man would have been the answer."

Elizita goes striding into the middle of her story, unfolding everything she has to tell us since she and Cecil lost contact, from just before they were married secretly and left for America.

"Will you *use* what I give you on the programme?" she asks me.

"Do you want me to? You can always change your mind."

"And what if you change yours? This is about you too, isn't it?" she says, lilting on the *yours*, and I am not sure if she means *you too* or *you two*.

I begin wondering about the mechanics, if anyone will be able to understand it without being told voice-over that Elizita married Cecil after she attempted to commit suicide.

In the school holidays, when he was young, Cecil worked for the town corporation at the town pool as a helper. Cecil's father was well heeled – if you considered how well, you might say it unbalanced Cecil. Making him feel both privileged and deprived, for his father gave Cecil no pocket money, insisting that Cecil earn it when he wasn't at school – at weekends and on holidays. Cecil said his job with the Council only taught him to stare longingly at El, who would plunge in naked along with Terry at 7:30 in the morning while the other girls in their pod swam backstroke in an assortment of bikini bottoms.

Cecil was too poor to afford a girlfriend, but the girls knew him to be the son of a millionaire.

"Go ahead, use everything I say and anything you see," says El. "It'll do them a power of good." Elizita pulls loose the belt of her silk robe and takes a silver bathing cap from the pocket. Once it tightens on her head, it makes her full lips stand out more. They are not red; they are, as they've always been, a prominent maroon. Her suit is a silver one-piece tied behind the neck with strings into a bow.

"Do who good?" Terry asks, and touches the corner of Elizita's mouth gingerly as if she thinks it has been hurt.

Elizita doesn't answer. She turns away from Terry and bends to run her finger round the heel of the rubber pool slipper, pulling it tighter. It strikes me that she has been standing here every morning since J. called and Terry spoke to her from Vancouver.

"Cecil was like you, Gavin." Elizita looks down her body, presumably to check it is all there. "Sensitive, attentive, but I didn't actually like it that much – it made me feel as if what I wanted was like an illness. Right enough, sex *was* a sickness I had, and Cecil hovered around it, thinking that what I needed was to be understood and cared for. But that was only the 'alf of it."

"The sensitive ones hover," says Terry, "like they want to tie your shoelaces so you won't trip." The remark surprises me into swinging the camera to Terry.

"Cecil should have known," Elizita says behind me, "from before, from when he and Sandy used to watch us girls rubbing oil into each other. Sometimes we girls like to be touched and not just looked at. And, sometimes we want to be watched and not touched."

As if to illustrate, Elizita moves to the edge of the pool and drops into the water before I can follow her with the camera. I am not particularly worried because I base a lot of the composition on natural counterpoint, which allows viewers to be seeing one thing while the commentary runs in another direction, but I do have Terry in focus by the time she plunges in behind Elizita. Their robes are left floating across a recliner and a chair. There is an oriental bath scene on one, Terry's, and on Elizita's – forms made out of shades of silver, a platinum sea of waves or what could be a sky full of striated clouds, where Elizita's face and body roll in the arms and between the hands of faceless silver-grey lovers.

I rest the camera on my shoulder with the viewer to my eye. Terry has taken Elizita by the shoulders and holds her from behind. She whispers in her ear and prevents her from turning in the direction of the camera for a moment or two.

Now, Terry moves both hands to El's hips, turns her, pulls her toward herself and grins, baring her teeth as close to El's face as she can without their two heads bashing. The water makes their movements slow and sweeping as though they are swinging round in the silks of their gowns, which sends off ripples that subside over the length of the pool.

"It's heaven," says Terry, following the roll of the water. Then, she looks at El very seriously. "Where did your lips and your bum come from – I always wanted to know…"

"I always told you, didn't I – '*A black mon and a black mum frum Burming-um?*' – It *is* called the Black Country, after all."

"On account of the soot."

"And the smut? Could be my father came back from somewhere he never talked about, before he came to Northern Ireland. Could be they adopted me off *sum black mum in Burming'um*. El is for Eliza, *hoo might uv'bin black*, but Zita – the name – is Hungarian. Could have been a gypsy who left me with my nametag on their doorstep. I don't know where I got my bits from."

"Where we all get it," Terry says as her hands slip down behind Elizita in the water. Terry looks into her face. El's teeth split through her lips in a smile. The two of them begin to turn again, hands on each other's hips, stirring and churning the early morning silk of the water with their arms.

"Some of us like legs, some of us like bellies."

"Some of us could suck shoulders, some of us the lot."

"I thought it was just me," El says when they stop. "The sun on me bum and the buzz between me legs. Remember I used to say, if only it were healthy!"

"If only it were healthy," Terry smiles at her until El's eyes wrinkle, but she looks suddenly sad, staring off at the bare land, blue sky, hills, as though finding the cause for some small sorrow there.

"Does what you do help?" Terry asks, her arms moving around Elizita, lifting to her shoulders, dropping to her waist.

"You mean, after I put my head in the gas oven over the sorry cases I had to attend to on the dole and Cecil saved me? Oversensitive Cecil. He had come by to invite me to a reception at Speckworthy's, where he was interning as a buyer for men's clothes. He was shouting for me and I was answering, shouting and choking myself on the gas, 'Wait till I'm done, luv.'

"He came in expecting to find me with my legs round someone like the sales clerk I had taken a fancy to, someone at Speckworthy's when I was in seeing Cecil. A sales clerk who was a bodybuilder and sold socks and ties. I couldn't wait to see him in just his socks and tie."

"Socks and thighs," Terry says, and Elizita erupts into a laugh. Terry's hands slip down to hold Elizita by the backs of hers.

"Well, there I was gassing myself, you daft nit. Cecil turns off the burners and looks into the oven at me. 'Do you want to come to this reception for the American and those other suppliers from across the water?'

"'Anyone *frum Burming'um*?' I want to know, 'or just the Americun?'

"'Don't know,' says Cecil, '*cum* and judge for yourself, luv, or carry on as you are.'

"Cecil didn't mean to be funny, but he was, and that stopped me.

"'Alright,' I says, 'I will,' and I sit up to vomit over the deck shoes he always has on, as if he's ready to go sailing."

Elizita's eyes are shining. Perhaps it is with the cold of the water and the light desert breeze blowing.

"And…?" Terry asks.

"There was someone at the do from Levi's." El puts her hand up to Terry's cheek, turning her face away from me, apparently, to whisper in her ear. But it is no whisper. "A fella from America, in Levi's and a sports coat, beaming with health and sexual mania. It was the sexual revolution and I thought I was in it on my own. Not able to get out of this feeling I was sick, not able to get out of it, not even through the gas oven door.

"Then, I met this Ham in the Levi's and the sports coat. They say sportcoat here. He's talking to me, and he has his gadget stood up to attention, or maybe it was at ease, behind the buttons of his fly. Buttons, not a zipper. He's getting volumes of sales off Cecil, and asking for Cecil's reaction to the cleats on his denim shirt. Cleats with pearl fronts that you can rip open. Buttons on his fly, and pearl cleats on his shirt. Cecil, he notices, has put on one of the samples he sent, but not with the pearl cleats, the plain metal ones with the Levi's name on them. 'You know this type of shirt I have is good for cowboys, or any working stiff. If they get torn open, no buttons are lost and none need sewing back,' says Ham. It's a Levi's shirt, but Cecil has a tie on and the Levi's shirt collar up to his ears, Lord love us, the way he used to with a dress shirt.

"The American undoes Cecil's tie and lets it hang, undoes Cecil's top button, which is the only real button on the shirt, then pulls the top three of his plain cleats open. Lord love us – Cecil has a chest! Remember his chest, he was so anxious most of the time, you could forget."

I sit down to relieve my back, which is beginning to hurt. Elizita has taken Terry's face in both her hands. "Remember, Terry, you used to brush his chest with your hand when you talked to him at the pool. Like it was polished, like you'd found little bits of dust on it."

Terry nods. "Lord, it was tight, but fine as silk. Supple, wouldn't you say?" I put down the camera only to jerk it back up again in case I have set it in water. I haven't looked to see.

"Just like the skin on his cock," Elizita says loud enough to see if it cuts me through my confusion with my precious camera.

"Ham, that's the name of the American, puts his hand in to lay it on Cecil's chest. 'There's something there, why not let it show?' says he. Why not? I'm turned on about Cecil's chest, but getting a headache, and getting quite nasty. I look at Ham's crotch and I ask, 'You like buttons down there?'

"'Some things are just too good to rush,' says he, screwing Cecil and me with his sales pitch, and Cecil is digging it more than I am. This Ham is screwing everybody with his eyes. He's supposed to be testing the taste of the local market, but know what this Ham was doing? Like most Americans, he was creating the taste, whetting the eyes of all and sundry.

"He winked and pushed Cecil's clasps back together, one by one. Everybody was looking at Ham, and the look he gave them back was like he'd just been to bed with all of them, but was about to leave without asking any of them for their hand in marriage."

Elizita puts her finger in her mouth to wet it with saliva and smooth each of Terry's eyebrows in turn until she's satisfied. "I still love your eyebrows, Terry. They always look as if they've been lacquered," she adds.

"Cecil's glossy tits and my eyebrows. Real – what is it – turn-ons?"

They talk idly now, as they did when they were younger, as if on this morning they have all the time in the world. Or is it for a purpose? To perhaps see if what they share will make me edgy. Word by languid word am I expected to shrink from sight, get lost in the camera or the composition of my commentary on something else, go and film the town of McNair, the Death and Amargosa Valleys, the water diviners, the geologists, out chipping away at those rocks that grow about like stone cacti in the middle of nowhere?

"We went to Acapulco," says Terry, "on a last-minuter for £800. To a hotel, the Caleta. There was this diver by the hotel on the rocks. Just light cotton trunks. The trunks tied so's his thing was crooked at you, like a finger, inviting you to come on over."

Terry puts her arm round Elizita's neck. "So, was that the last of Ham?"

I look round, needing to relieve my eyes. Staring into an uninhibited conversation causes vertigo. An identical dizziness to when we stopped on the road to McNair. I leaned out over the wall to see into a canyon and follow two eagles that could have been buzzards, spiralling down and away. I leaned out farther and farther to catch a last glimpse of the birds and almost fell in behind my camera. Terry was worried for me, but not now.

The women spiral and spiral, and I attribute it to something deranged about the light and the sun here. I begin to ponder it melodramatically to distract myself, but the thoughts only turn in a circle with the women. It is neither winter, nor summer light, nor spring, nor autumn's – it is warm, it goes on brazenly making Terry and Elizita expose themselves in a way that the summers would make them do at home, but in a hard way, a barren way, as if the naked honesty of the stone all around here has put on the women's skin and wants to touch everything in the most intimate place, to gauge the depth of flesh, the extent of feeling.

"We drove Ham round to the Royal Avenue Hotel from Speckworthy's. What would we like as a thank-you?

Stand-up or a sit-down drink at the bar or in his room? It's late and the barman is somewhere, looking to replace a bottle. Cecil needs to pee and I'm left with Ham. Ham takes his hands and lifts up my dress. I pull my knickers down to my knees. I drop them, step over them, give them to him. He puts them in the pocket of his sportcoat like they're my calling card.

"Americans say *sportcoat*, remember."

Terry bats her eyelashes together in mock ditziness. "I'm gushing with nostalgia for the old Royal Avenue Hotel," she says. "We always wanted to stay there on RAG night after the RAG ball at Queen's."

"My problem is I want my whole life like RAG nights after the RAG ball," says Elizita. "I like it wild, but I like it organized."

"Like America," I say, but am not listened to.

"We used to watch you," says Terry, "the times you actually used the changing boxes at the pool. Those were great peek-a-boo doors that covered you from shoulder to knee. We'd see your pants go up, then come back down again when you put on your skirt. You kept them in your school bag, didn't you, on those days?"

"Didn't we keep all the important stuff in our school bags?" Elizita asks, and she and Terry slap the surface of the water with the flat of their hands.

"Lord, that night my lips stuck to Cecil's tits like limpets," Elizita says sadly, and looking down at her body, which is soaked from the splashing; without another word, she begins to swim laps, leaving Terry to watch, then follow her.

Have they been waiting for someone other than me, the waiter who they see coming along the side of the pool, to stop their reminiscing? They swim away dismissing me, leaving me beside the waiter, who nods and watches them swimming together. He waits patiently, looking at the camera as I drop it wearily to my side.

Seeing them so solidly together in their bodies and their conversation, I am as confused as I used to be at the poolside back home. Is their duet in the water to let me watch their legs and arms, instead of listening to them? I remember how they used to stand, wiping the sweat from their stomachs after lying on the wooden planks that served as seats on the bleachers, then dive into the ridiculous milkiness of the pool.

They would take a breath before diving in. A small prayer in the intake before the heart-jolting switch from hot to cold. When they came up, they swam in another element, another existence that was made entirely of light, air, water and limbs.

When they swam back to the side wall, it was to look up out of the water at me standing on the bank. My toes would curl over the concrete edge as I looked into the cleft between their breasts and I would get vertigo.

Elizita taps my foot with her painted fingernail. She shakes her head at the waiter and he leaves. Her nipples in the silver racing slip stand out, but the full contours of her breasts are pressed down by it. They look elastic and young. Terry has stopped behind her; she comes up, puts her hands through Elizita's arms and onto each breast.

"Diddies groped," she lets out one of their ritual vulgarities.

"Grope Gavin's, he has them too," Elizita says to my face. "A bit heavy now, and soft." Her eyes query me for confirmation. "Drooping at the nipples?"

"How do you like your nipples?" Terry prolongs the litany into the order of tits.

"Big and ripe. Cold, too – my dear, like strawberries on a sundae." Elizita has her order of nipples ready on the instant.

"When I first came to America, I loved sundaes. Ham was always eating them. He wanted Cecil over in Salt Lake City after we got married. To see the land Levi's come from. Ham wasn't Mormon, but he liked the idea of the Mormons. He used to say if he could only get them to give up the dark suits and go round the world preaching in denim for Levi's, they'd make a fortune for the company. Then, he imagined them doing it for this other outfit called Vaquero's.

"Ham set me up in the railway repair yard, but…" she looks up into my bared face, where the camera was a moment before, "Gordie got me started."

We remember Gordie. He was gruff and worked for the Belfast County Down Railway, part of Ulster Transport, as it was called then. He had a degree, but you'd have thought he'd learned everything with his hands and a spanner. He wanted to have a factory of his own, any kind of factory. Didn't matter if it manufactured candies or brass rings.

Now, this is how I begin imagining this Ham she tells us about. We nod, Terry and I, with agreement over a puzzlement Terry shares with me, and some alarm that Terry has not anticipated. The mention of Gordie has broken the unison in the female mischief and reminiscing.

"Gordie liked you, Terry… Gordie," Elizita repeats his name, pushes it at Terry, then, leaves it hanging. Terry turns to me to let me see her unpreparedness regarding Gordie. But I am doubly sure this is the way she imagines Ham, in the way we remember Gordie, working with his toolbox, a screwdriver or spirit level sticking out of a breast pocket in his overalls for show, his face butted forward, eyeing you like *you* were where he would put his oil can next.

"Gruff Gordie?" Terry and I say it together.

"Lord luv yuh. Gruff made me feel at home. Trouble up mill, man in charge of works, getting sommut fixed," says Elizita. "On the ten o'clock train between the Holywood and Helen's Bay stop, Gordie fixed me. I was thirteen and I thought I was mad. He was only twenty-four, you know. It feels like no difference now. Then, it felt like I was fucking my father and couldn't wait for the train to get out of Helen's Bay station to have more before it stopped in Carnalea."

"Always wore a brown Harris tweed sports coat, after work. Grey worsted pants," I say, as he comes to mind better…

"Did you go out on that bike of his after work?" Elizita asks me.

I did. I remember how he had checked me automatically, getting off, to see what his Triumph Bonneville had worked up, if it was properly tuned.

"Never put on a helmet in his life. Always managed to do the ton for me," Elizita sighs.

"Is this railroad, repair yard thing to do with Gordie?" I ask.

"Only coincidentally. It's what Ham wanted me to run to begin with, a museum to hold old rolling stock, passenger cars and some locomotives. Maybe rent them later like they do at one of those places in Reno, but a lot of gambling went on in them instead, and a little bit of t'other too."

"Did Gordie ever take off his sports coat?" I ask.

"He did," says Elizita, "but his arms and legs were hairy. Made of the same Harris tweed as his coat." El pulls herself out of the water. "Remember, Terry, the peeler stopping us for being three up on Gordie's bike?" Elizita turns to help Terry up out of the water by her elbows, turning her with them, like a doll, putting her arms round her from behind to talk into her ear.

"Cold?" she asks.

"I can feel my goosebumps turning into nipples," Terry says over her shoulder to Elizita.

Elizita whispers something, a few details about the repair yard being an hour or half-hour's drive away. Then, she grins, drops her hands to Terry's hips to grip them, riding an invisible pillion with her, jerking as if she changes gear, bumping Terry's rear end, driving her toward me.

"Is Cecil still in Salt Lake City?" Terry asks over her shoulder when their two faces come close-up to the camera.

Elizita laughs. "He could be, for all I hear from him. I told you he thought his being nice turned me on, saved my life, but it was an accident and I took it for fate bringing me the right man at the right time. For a while I told him all about my agonies, about how Gordie damaged me, but not how Gordie also made me permanently horny. If the first time you fuck it's for fuck's sake, love gets separated, lost in a different slot. Then, Ham comes right in and hauls Cecil by the crotch of his Levi's to Salt Lake City. And how can I tell Cecil it's the same for him as for me? Recruited by the crotch."

"Let me get this properly." I want El to repeat it clearly after me. "If I am correct, you came to Salt Lake City on a honeymoon business trip. I know you did marry Cecil. In Salt Lake, while visiting Levi's, this Ham offers Cecil a job running a Vaquero's operation. Is that the word they use — operation?"

"Of course. Weren't you listening?" Terry scolds me.

I am squinting through the sun in the direction of El's hands winding my wife into her wrap. The waiter appears out of the sun for her, a movement from one of Elizita's hands, or the putting on of the wrap itself must have summoned him.

"Time for some orange juice, or how would Buck's Fizz hit you – to celebrate?"

"Pitcher of Buck's Fizz with a squeeze of lime, Bryan," she says to the waiter without waiting for an answer.

"Yes, Ms. L," he says.

That's all the waiter says.

"For business and all transactions I'm L. Easier to be L over here. Elizita is just a bit too Mexican, although it's not bad if they think that. A Mexican with a *Burming'um* accent."

Owning one letter of the alphabet that everybody here knows is hers – not just a few friends like us, who said *El* like a single *L* for the snob sound of it – naturalizes Elizita, makes her American. We might mock it, but admire her instead, all the more for it.

"Do you live in this museum for old rolling stock and locomotives?" I ask. "L's, is it?"

"I'm L, but the place is E-L's. Sure is," Elizita clarifies. "The business name, EL's, really starts with Vaquero's World here in the U.S., Mundo Vaquero in Latin America. After Cecil learns the ropes for the Vaquero franchises. This is in '72 or '73, round about there. Ham puts him forward as the person to set up a test outlet, a boutique in Mexico City. Ham will pass the outfitting of the store and the training of the Mexican who owns the franchise on to Ces, then Ces can do the same in the other cities.

"*Ces* is what Ham always calls Cecil because he insists on being called as he always was, Cess-ill, and not See-sill. Ham cuts that one to Ces, puts Ces on a plane permanently and humps me till his heart's content.

"Ces is in Chile now, owns a vineyard. He just doesn't have it in him to come back. That's the deal."

I am listening to Elizita say *deal*, admiring the American way of saying it in her North Country accent, but her mouth isn't English, her mouth and her teeth and her jaw are like Cleo Laine's. There's a great heartiness when Elizita laughs and always, as it did before, it makes me want to put my ear to her chest to hear if it's as genuine inside as it appears to be outside where it booms at you.

The Buck's Fizzes – champagne and orange juice with a squeeze of lime – arrive. Hardly one moment after Terry has drunk it back, she is touching me in front of Elizita. Doing it for Elizita to look at. But I force back the urge to shift away, pretending not to feel the touch of Terry's fingers until I get up to take a higher angle on Elizita's head as she talks.

Elizita straightens her back as she sits on the metal chair, which is painted stark white. Its seat is topped with a green circular cushion. She talks, leans back, lifting her breasts, drawing me toward her as she does – to make me feel that at any moment I might topple onto her lap, wriggling and giggling as I did years ago. I could as easily be lying, mumbling to her thighs instead of listening to her.

I have to sit down again.

Now, it's Terry, perhaps mimicking me, moving back and forth in front of us, dipping all the time while she speaks to a still-reclining Elizita, or to me where I have sat down to keep from falling. Terry holds herself over us, her hands resting on our shoulders, a squeeze going with everything she says, as if her hands are the words, kneading what she wants to get across with her body into us. The closer she gets, the more fervent she is about how good it is being here, in touch at last, the more she leans over, the more I feel she wants to lower her breasts into my mouth or Elizita's. It is obscenely solicitous, but Terry does this deliberately. "Gavin says the camera reads body language. That's his business, Elizita. And I'm letting my body speak for what I can't on this gorgeous morning."

Terry leans her face all the way down to Elizita's. Elizita reaches her hands around the back of Terry's neck, holds her head to steady her, then kisses her.

I'm almost angered into a lecture about my job to avoid deciding if Elizita kisses fondly or the other way. "For my part, I need to see that my body isn't doing the talking, or the lens will miss the point." I get up, pick up where I left off, following their every move. "I'll carry the camera and you two carry on the conversation. Okay?"

They burst out laughing, and it acts as the correction I need. In the process of doing a programme where one is personally involved, constant self-reminding about cutting oneself out is required. And that the personal and the public can be separated in the editing room.

Elizita has picked up on her story.

"I keep asking Ham — why Salt Lake City? He has his answer: 'Piety and a slim possibility of polygamy, plus it gets so hot folks can't bear much underwear. Denim coveralls, that's it. American Gothic in smocks, and coveralls, nothing underneath but good honest sweat. You can put your hand right in the pocket of any mechanic's coveralls and feel his ball bearings. That turn you on, L?'

"Yes, he was the first to call me L, here. Just like Cess-ill, Ces."

Elizita looks at Terry.

Terry licks her lips. "I like the ads for jeans," Terry says. "Bare bellies, and the zipper undone as far as it will go, without…"

"Getting pubic hair caught in it, 'cause there ain't any – all shaved off. So, Terry – my darlin', that's what you think of those young men models – male flowers for the masses. A pretty little flash of the pubis flesh, but not the awful, little lizard thing, hiding behind the flies on those eye-candy lads."

Terry shuts her eyes and opens her mouth to the sun.

"You're beginning to burn," Elizita warns her. She takes sunscreen from the pocket of her gown and gets up, pulls down the straps of Terry's swimsuit and Terry's hands immediately go up to her breasts, but Elizita is already applying the screen to her shoulders.

"You're beginning to burn too," she tells me. She puts her fingertip to a freckle on my shoulder. "You're hairier here than you used to be." She touches the backs of my arms and my belly with the backs of her own fingers, moving along the hairs, missing the skin. "Can't see any freckles here anymore," she says, looking at my stomach, "but at least it doesn't stick out."

I am embarrassed by being glad of this opinion. Terry has taken out a comb from the pocket of her gown and is running it through her hair, looking at us as she strokes the hair back from her brow. Elizita winks, then takes the comb that Terry offers her, puts her hand over the camera and combs my hair.

"Still there," she says.

Again, I am stupidly glad and set the camera on the table, but don't enter into the conversation. I leave the camera running, aimed at where Elizita goes into recliner mode again.

"Ham thought Ces would look good in an ad. Ces was keen on them and wanted to get onto the board that made the decisions about which ones to run. Ces goes on at Ham for months about this. 'You don't start at the end, Ces,' says Ham, 'you come in on the idea for one. At the first pitch, dummy. Easier if we do a dummy run…' Ham likes doing this, doubling up on the dummy bit. 'I'll rustle up one of the creative types and a photographer to let you see the process.' In next to no time he turns up at the house with two birds. One in slacks, white shirt, black hair and black briefcase, black club-heel shoes, along with the other, a blonde carrying a heavy overnight bag full of lenses and light meters and a camera like yours, Gavin. Good for stills and live action."

Elizita laughs into the camera.

"As soon as they're in the door, Ham is asking, 'Take a good look. Think Ces will do for the job?' Before either of them answer, the creative type points and asks a question of her own. 'That the wall-wide window with the view of the desert you talked about? What I want is him – Ces, is it? – against the windowpane, like he's falling out of the sky, and into the desert. He's a bit like David Bowie, right? Man-Who-Fell-From-the-Sky look for the Sky-Blue line.' Camera Girl gives Ces the once-over while Ms. Creative lays the scene. 'Good shoulders, cool butt, great abdominals, natural gleam off the pecs,' says Camera Girl. 'Won't need a drop of oil,' she says to Ms. Creative while looking at Ces, head to bare feet, in Sky-Blue Vaquero denims. Camera Girl pulls Ces's shirt out of his trousers, rips apart the cleats with a pop and pats him on the rear end. 'Don't get too stiff with her,' says Ham, 'she's a photographer, just doing her job, like I told you.' Camera Girl's fussing with the shirt, pulling at the front tails so the buttonholes on one side and the cleats on the other hang past the tips of his nipples. Then she asks him if he can hold that, back up, put his butt against the glass and spread his legs and arms out against it, flat as he can, too. 'You got that stepping stool I asked for?' Ms. Creative asks Ham. 'We need him higher up in the window for the backdrop,' she tells Camera Girl, and they grin at each other at what kind of backdrop it could be if the window doesn't hold. Then, she yells over her shoulder for Ham who's coming with a powder-blue-painted stepping stool. 'This window strong enough to take him splayed up against it?' 'Strong enough to take a tornado,' Ham yells back. 'You wish,' says Camera Girl, as she takes a comb to the blond hair on Ces's belly, stroking it into a mane running up from his crotch to his belly button. Ces's crotch is in full sail by now. 'I'd leave you to it, but this is getting interesting,' says Ham, and falls back onto the leather couch beside me, arms up, like he's dropped out of the sky."

"You were there, you saw all this?" Terry turns from where she has spread herself on the recliner beside Elizita, and asks my question for me. I come closer to catch Elizita's concentration as she remembers.

"Yep. Sure as a cum frum Burming'um, Ms. Creative backs up and sits right there on the other side of Ham on the leather couch, like both of us aren't there. Then, Ham wiggles his butt between us, but I get to see Ms. Creative's folder, which she has been holding out front of her like a hymnal in the choir. It's open over a shot of Bowie in *The Man Who Fell to Earth* and a photo of Ces at the pool, back of the house, Ham must have given her. 'Is this a dummy run?' I ask her, and she gives me a look that really makes me feel I'm not there, then, this smile like she's suddenly registered this other bird in the room and likes what she sees. She nods to Ham, 'Good choice.'

"Ms. Creative gets up to go stand behind Camera Girl. Sure enough, Ces sprawls against that window and doesn't smash down through it into the desert for real. Lots of shots, lots of repositionings until Camera Girl turns to Ms. Creative and clicks her through what she's got. They nod.

"'Turns me on,' says Ms. Creative. 'Me, too,' I say to Ham.

"Camera Girl, she has an idea for another spread. Ces has to take the jeans off, hang them over his arm so the camera will catch his bare legs and hips on either side of the jeans. He keeps the shirt on, open.

"'Like you give birth to the folded Sky-Blues from your very own belly,' says Ms. Creative. 'An offer to the men out there to take them and put them on – the guys, I mean,' says Ms. Creative.

"'Invitation for the lady friend is just to take them off the guy, as offered. We got to get those outside curves on the hips that will make a woman want to grab, so no boxers or that ugly bullshit. Off with them.'

"Ces complies. Who wouldn't?"

"Bet you wouldn't!" Terry taunts me.

"Remember I'm Camera Guy. You're good at this, Elizita, telling it like it is."

"Bare naked," says Terry, and chokes on the bottom of the Buck's Fizz, which she has overly upended toward her mouth.

"Don't quip with your mouth full, Terry – as Ms. Mathers would say at the girls' Collegiate."

"Shall I continue? Ces pulls off his jeans, hopping to get his legs out and turns away to yank off his bullshit underwear. We'd get a rear-end view, but Camera Girl stands close behind him to block it, but holds both hands out on either side like she's going to plant them on his butt cheeks.

"Ces folds the jeans as neatly as he does afore he goes to bed. 'Always folds his jeans,' I say to Ms. Creative, who tells Camera Girl, 'Keep the window behind him, move all that stuff from in front of it. We want just him, walking out of the desert with his Vaquero's folded over his arms,' says Ms. Creative, who comes and lowers her rear slowly on the couch on the other side of Ham again while she keeps her eye on the set-up as Camera Girl pops behind Ces to do the clearing.

"She slaps him on the bare butt when she goes back to the camera.

"'Good job,' says Ms. Creative, to put an end to the shoot.

"Ham turns to me, but says to Ms. Creative, 'You can pay anybody to do anything in America, and they'll give it all they've got. The pay makes it a pure joy.'

"'What about Ces?' I yelp. 'He's doing this for zip.'

"'Don't get your Brummie back up,' says Ms. Creative while all three, Ms. Creative, Camera Girl and Ham look at me, then Ces.

"I'd hate the bitch for knowin' that where I cum frum makes me a Brummie if she didn't go and add, 'He'll be paid in kind. Bare-assed kind.'

"'That turn you on?" she asks me.

"'Exchange of that kind allus does.' What 'bout you, Terry… no need to answer.

"Back to the excitement. Ces fell in love with the photographer. Saw her everywhere he went in Latin America for Vaquero's. They're probably fucking each other as I speak, in his vineyard, east of Valparaiso. Oh, yes. Set himself up there he did."

Pulling at the front of her swimsuit and pushing her fresh glass of Buck's Fizz between her breasts, Terry turns to Elizita.

"And Ces leaves you in Salt Lake City with Ham humping you, and Ms. Creative, till his heart's content?"

The question is let ride. "Cum up and see," says Elizita, "I have a permanent suite here at the Clear Haven. We'll leave, later. No need for you to drive. Park the car here."

"Leave for where?"

"El's Railroad," she answers. "Where else? One thing I can guarantee about it, rent's free. But, sex isn't."

"Ham know we're coming?" Terry asks, suddenly polite, and Elizita comes over, leans down and looks into her face.

"I'll have to write and find out. He's doing time." Elizita runs her hand over Terry's thigh, brushing away nothing but sunlight.

"You're kidding about the sex?" I ask.

"No, you pay in kind, like Ms. Creative said. Or in cash," she adds matter-of-factly.

"Screwing used to be a heartache, now it's part of the trade. Ham really did want me as Madam Manager for his museum. To set me up, he'd pay half in money he borrowed from a friend, half he filched from Vaquero's. Joint venture, good economics – cost-sharing.

"Vaquero's didn't see how he used their money same way he did. And his buddy, Bunny, who gave him the other half, said he didn't trust him, and would take me as collateral. He had a kinda cravin' for me as the madam of a railroad museum, too.

"Frank as can be was Bunny. Starting with him, Bunny wanted me to pay for Ham's half in bed – if ou't went wrong. He'd send others to build business in the casino cars and cathouse-cum-caboose.

"'Always wanted to own a fucking train,' says Bunny, 'but that's not what we'll call it. We'll call it El's Railroad, after you – sound good? The El *is* yours and not an alias?' says Bunny, ''cause I like it, see – El's Railroad. Long ago, I seen this caption on a Nevada billboard: *Come on in to WHAT-CAT-AND-MAN-DO, where miners can work off their wages in sin.* I like things catchy.'

"Bunny pays Vaquero's off for their embezzled stake in El's Railroad. They want nothing to do with a legal brothel in Nevada; and after Ham is inside for five years, Bunny gives it to me anyway. Couldn't use it no more. Decided to climb aboard me one night, then he got off and shot himself before he couldn't remember who I was or what he was doing. In his opinion, and who's to argue, a hood with Alzheimer's is no good. There, I told you in good plain American, my story. Randy Burming'um girl makes good just lying on her bum."

"You didn't freak out?" Terry asks, and I look at Terry as startled by her word choice as by what Elizita has told us.

"Does it freak you out?" Elizita asks back.

Freak is the kind of word Terry is leery of, as if in saying it she might expose herself to something of it in herself. Under her linguist's dispassionate, academic cool, Terry's attitude to language is superstitious. I know she has avoided mentioning Elizita, in many ways, because mentioning her would arouse the old tearaway times. The side of Terry, or me, that Gruff Gordie took for a spin on the back of his bike, and we kept hidden from each other. The side that starts, not with love, but a fuck, for fuck's sake, and gets confused.

I watch Elizita touch a drop of water that hasn't dried on Terry's shoulder with her finger. The drop has fallen from the wet ends of her hair, which Elizita takes in a towel and begins drying.

"Come on, did I actually freak you out or turn you on, Terry?"

"The way you talk about selling sex, Elizita…"

"That turn you on?"

"I'm curious. Interested in how you say what you say. Just when it gets wet and exciting for me, it turns and sounds matter-of-fact for you."

"You're a linguist, you should be the first to understand that. If sex is your business, talk about it business-like. But I'm glad you got wet twice."

It's easy too to forget that Terry became Terr, i.e. Tear, aka, tearaway.

It's only when we get drunk that we return to that girl. This is one of those times. At school she passed everyone else in her set in being precocious, ahead of them in every department, except real sex – I believed. Lover of gesture, the body linguist, who gave no content to her vocabulary, whereas Elizita would always end up doing everything she said or thought or imagined. Everything, even if it meant having a bun, or her head, stuck in the oven.

Long before I started this programme, I tried to define Terry and her tribe at the Collegiate. The closest I have come to a definition is "renewable virgins." They have to be won round again, wooed each time after they have made love, as if they possess no memory of the last time they were aroused. How can I describe it? They are as virgin after passion has passed, as unruffled as the water when the wind has died. Their composure closes over everything, sealing them into a renewed assurance of their beauty and desirability, their impenetrability.

For me, their bodies were always connected to the sea – now, sexily, inextricably confused with the backdrop of a pool in the American desert.

When I stopped the car in the Amargosa, I had the same sense of recognition and enormous inertia, the certainty that there had never been any movement made by me over its dust and sand. Outside, it felt exactly the same when I lay on the back seat of the car between Terry's thighs, post-passion, with the engine and the air-conditioning on. I knew I might just as well have been outside sweating between the hot fenders of the rental, looking up the road through the heat waves at the desert.

I blame my work all over again for the separation. I feel I haven't even touched her, but as soon as someone else lays a finger on her, I feel it pass through her to me at the same time. The same with the desert. I felt the whole scope of it as soon as I saw the dust trail of another car cross it on a dirt road in the opposite direction while I stood watching. The same with the sea, with the water in the pool here at the Clear Haven, the moment Terry and Elizita break the tension of the water, they swim through me – Terry and her set, her whole generation and class of women, with the two of them. Outrageously forward and elusive – exclusive.

As girls, they stripped gladly to leap into the sea when they believed their bare skin was the only skin touching it. In the sixties, when hippies made the mad baring of mind and body common, it sent theirs into mourning. The unwashed discovering the sun blazing on their skin and inside their heads at the same time amused, then offended. Here, in America, I realize why so many of them have come across – whatever it is, everybody has a right to the virgin experience. And at the same time I feel that you can try to screw the desert till you're blue in the face and you won't even leave an impression.

I watch Elizita let Terry's hair drop out of the towel in her hands and her look at it. "You need to be paid attention to," she says to Terry, then asks her, "Would you…?"

"Would I what?"

Elizita lifts Terry's robe and drapes the silk men in the tub and the women on their knees around her shoulders.

Hand on Terry's shoulders, she rubs them lightly, lifting the silk, letting it drop, not actually rubbing at all.

There was a leaf off a particular hedge, which we used to place on the backs of our hands while we rubbed dust and gravel from the road over it. It would stick to the skin and when we peeled it off, the flesh underneath would be clear white and pungent with the smell of the leaf, and the pattern of the veins would be left, a pale skeleton over the open, faintly sweating pores of the hand.

In the room when I stand in front of her and hold back her robe I expect to see marks…that the men in the tub have slipped from the silk and are branded on Terry's back and between her breasts, their heads bobbing up and down there. I want to put my mouth and hands in among theirs – can she feel that when I touch her?

Elizita could before we left the pool deck, in spite of the camera held like a cross to ward off a luscious vampire.

On the road, in El's convertible, I begin to think about something else: beyond the primping, the prompting and priming, even as girls Terry and the troop at the old tidewater pool slyly preened darling, daring Elizita, knowing how beyond the good, acceptable boys, there were bad rips, but good-lookers they could groom Elizita for and learn all about through her. The ones El would sail by with in the dark, acknowledging with a lift of the hand and small movement of the fingers that she saw, had been seen by her twittering klatch. Unable to hold back, Elizita kissed in full view under the lamp, directly down the steps from their school-house at the pool's front entrance, excited, driven by the hands of the boy, the looks of her friends. They pooled their teenage prurience in her, back then.

Now, the clanging of an engineer's bell isn't wildly advertising a train's going by, but greeting Elizita, who stands on the seat of the convertible in her bare feet while the restrained orange and greens of the railcars pass by, shaking and shuddering over the crossing. El slips down into the seat, smiling.

"Will that keep them on their toes or on their backs?" Elizita asks Terry, as she places her feet back into the straps of the high heels on the carpeted floor. "The yard isn't far."

The red Impala convertible turns to run parallel to the track now. "Not a speck of rust," she says of the car. "Desert air. Good for the lungs and old automobiles."

There is parking all around the corrugated railway yard, where a caboose and three Pullmans sit, the tail end of a train outside the repair bay or roundhouse. The white markings for the parking berths and direction signs blaze off the black tarmac outside.

"You can fly in, if you care to."

Elizita sees we have noticed a landing strip with pot lights to mark it in the night. These blue ground lights which Elizita says she always imagines as the footlights for her big shows.

"There's nothing more exciting than seeing the naked fuselage of a plane when someone important is landing inside it," she says. "Like a god coming down from the sky with a hard-on just for you. Oh, about coming in... Two things I want from everybody coming from abroad, a passport and a medical certificate dated *now* – though we do do very thorough inspections on-site. You'd be surprised who turns out to be the dirtiest."

"A medical certificate for someone to get into a museum?" Terry asks coyly, opening the door on her side of the car only to be led through another in the corrugated wall of the railway yard. "Wouldn't a death certificate to verify them as a historical figure be better?"

Terry's joke is eclipsed by the shadow inside. It slants down beneath the sunlight that blazes from a row of tall windows higher up. There's this sense of being in an industrial palace, a small cathedral for rolling stock, where one pays and is transported.

The flat platforms around the rails and turntables inside are meant to receive the vehicles rather than passengers. In this iron-and-glass arcade, three turntables attach to three tracks that splice into outgoing and incoming railroad lines. Operations are controlled by a switching house with levers, dials, large buttons on a console for the expanded facilities of the original roundhouse and repair bay. Vintage cars have been uncoupled and lined up on the track, not all first class, but brilliantly preserved. The fork for that track runs from one turntable, out of the repair bay to an old-style station platform. Its wooden sign says in white paint, ELVILLE.

"We have fuck tours, or family-only tours, boarding for family further down the line."

Elizita points at the centre turntable with a caboose sitting on it.

"My office is at the tail end of the train," Elizita points it out. "My guard's van," she says, not using the American word, which I like better because it makes me feel I am where I am. *Guard's van* reminds me of the dismal shout of my youth, boarding on my way to school, the guard shouting past the closing doors whatever expression took him on the day: "Everybody on!" "All aboard!" Missing that train was as miserable as catching it. A journey out on the grey mornings and in with the anemic light of the evening. *Caboose* for me sounds like and goes with moose, buffalo or bison: a creature out of the Wild West, and the great beast of the railroad that terrified the Indian tribes with the sparks belching from its nostrils.

We mount the iron steps of the caboose on the turntable. "This is my lazy Susan," says Elizita. "I give it a spin for my visitors." On cue, it turns, taking us around for a panorama of the facility from the tailgate. "The choice of cake I have is simple," she digs Terry with her elbow, "beef or cheese. Would you believe it that the railway brings in as much money as t'other."

When Terry doesn't follow up on this small provocation, I ask El to tell me more about her railway.

"I needed the right locomotives and cars, and a run through a gold mine at the other end. You can pretend you're a miner, eighty or a hundred years ago. Lucky for me, I've been into railways and finance for a long time, compliments of Ham and Gordie."

"Ham and Gordie sounds like a sandwich, Elizita," Terry observes without the wrinkle of a smile. "Just the one for your lazy Susan."

Elizita smirks and shouts "Maisie! Maisie!" through the glass panel in a wooden door at the back of the caboose. She turns the brass handle on the door to open it, only to find herself shouting into the face of a woman behind it.

"Coffee, tea? Dry martini, milk?" Maisie asks immediately as we come in. Maisie's smile is full and forthcoming, no sign of sarcasm in it to go with her question.

Elizita's mouth opens and her great teeth come on.

"Guess?" she says to Maisie.

"Martini for you two ladies, coffee for the gentleman?"

She tries to catch sight of my face behind the camera. I apologize, I daren't miss this first entrance to Elizita's office.

"Coffee," I confirm.

"Let me present my friends, Terry and Gavin. Terry and Gavin, this is Maisie, my exec."

I nod, but encumbered with the camera, my head goes up and down more slowly, moving my whole body with it, like a hunchback's. Once the introductions are done, Maisie kisses Terry on the cheek.

"Exec just means I do what she tells me." Maisie's explanation causes Terry to pause until Terry decides to kiss her back, heartily.

We have stepped into an early nineteen-hundreds' office. Rolltop desks with computers built in. Oak typing chairs with dark blue velvet cushions, Persian carpet and a single incongruity: some strange, posturepedic stool for the back that would let one lock one's feet behind it and rock back and forth like a penitent. I wonder who uses it.

"Did I agree to a martini?" Terry asks Maisie, who is opening a fridge, fronted by a wooden door to make it resemble an icebox. "What time is it?" Terry asks, hoping it is deep enough into the p.m. to forgive herself the tipple.

Elizita laughs and picks up the bone-handled phone from its cradle and dials.

"Time I called John… John, will you come and take Terry to her half-car? Yes, she's the one from school. And her husband, yes. You can look after him too, if he lets you."

Maisie holds open the icebox door with her shoulder and removes a silver cocktail canister from the aluminium interior, puts it into the crook of her arm, and at the same time, reaches to take two fresh martini glasses from it between her fingers.

"Martinis in the morning are a husband's warning," says Maisie, and pours.

"If you'll excuse me, I just want to look at the Barter Book. I always like to see if I recognize the names."

Elizita has already booted up and is scrutinising the screen.

"Half or whole, this is how the cars are rented. For you, a half-car is on the house."

"Well, since you are paying," says Terry, cheekily, her glass raised to the level of her brow in a salute to Elizita's gift or to squint through it.

"That's right, half is on me, but if you want it, you'll have to pay for t'other…" Elizita picks up her glass, turns from the screen and eyes Terry through her martini glass "…with someone other than each other."

From the look on John who has come in, he's not going to enlighten us on what Elizita has just proposed. He has laid our bags down on the back platform of the caboose and he is black. He stands oddly correct, his shoulders held square, as if lined up with the suitcases he set outside. He positively bristles with patience as he stands and waits without speaking.

"Don't stand with those big muscles humped up round your neck, as if you're still carrying those damn things you dumped outside. We'll all trip over them, you know, you know?" Elizita says, echoing Ena Sharples's sidekick from early *Coronation Street* on the BBC, but smiling with clear affection for the black man.

John doesn't witness this. He glances back at the cases, as if they have been wrongly tagged, and he has made yet another mistake that Elizita hasn't twigged on to yet.

"And where do *you* come from, John?" Terry asks.

Terry's plain butter-and-toast tone annoys me bad enough in the morning, but mulled with a martini and her spreading extra smarm on it because John is black gets my goat. That is, till I get a good look at her face. From that, I can't tell if she's being over-polite, or simply turned on by the big man, like she was, still is – by rugby players.

"There are no casuals," Elizita tells the lens on my shoulder, and she turns to read through a sheet of computer printout on her desk. "It's all cash or kind."

She stands up, comes around the camera to look at me, then goes and strokes Terry's hair from her face so that she can see Terry's eyes, which haven't left John while Terry waits for John to answer her curiosity about his origins.

"Montreal, I suppose," he says. "Mother was Haitian and my dad from Indiana. He came and dragged me out of junior high to Quebec because he had big objections to the war. And me, I was with the Alouettes, they're dead now."

By the time he has explained which war, the Vietnam, and that the Montreal Alouettes were a team playing in the Canadian Football League and that they failed financially and folded, Terry is touching his arm, sympathetically.

"Any two will do," says Elizita.

"One pays for t'other, if they can find a taker. It's a little gambling tool we've added to the trade," Elizita explains. "Customer coin toss that needs to land a second head or tail to win."

Once again her fingers go to Terry's hair, drawing it back from her face so that Terry can look directly at John or John at her. Her fingers trickle down under Terry's cheek a second time, as though checking the set of the jaw and lining up her profile for me to film.

Then, she turns to go over and put the same two fingers she placed on Terry's face on the sheet of figures she has just looked at.

"Three confirmed and two pending for today and tomorrow," she reads out in John's direction.

"American football player," Terry tilts her empty martini glass. "Very big and burly American football player. I'm so glad I've met one," Terry says, touching the shoulder of John's white cotton shirt.

"Canadian – once."

"Big broad John. With all his moving parts in the right places," says Elizita, smiling at me lusciously, because of the flush on my forehead, the first sign my blood is rising.

"The Alouettes," I say, and aim the camera directly at John.

"Yeah, great team. Great city."

"I bet you went down good with the Montrealers."

Elizita looks into my camera directly and tut-tuts Terry. "When a grammar school girl's grammar goes, her knickers are down round her ankles."

Terry lays one hand on John's shoulder to hold herself steady while she laughs. "Ms. Mathers at Collegiate would love to have said that."

"Knickers?" John asks, shaking his head. "Like guys wear to ride racing bikes?"

"Like girls take off to ride...oh, Jesus," says Terry.

John blinks at Terry's hand which has tightened on his shoulder. "You guys say weird things, we say some too. Bet if I said I got sacked a lot of times with the Alouettes, you'd think I was fired over and over, like?"

"*Sure*," says Terry, liking the way she says sure. I can tell.

"Doesn't mean that. On the field it means I got tackled and taken down."

"Around the legs, like rugby."

"Head-on, more like."

I put down the camera and tell Elizita, "You always know how to put us in a pickle."

"I like vinegar on my French fries," Elizita answers as John exits to pick up the suitcases. Terry follows him, talking to the back of his head and shoulders, the white sweep of the fine cotton shirt with the faint lining of black absorbing her completely.

Elizita pulls up the bottom window of the caboose, to let in some air…or for me to poke my head out and do some filming.

"First time through a new situation means a lot of camera," I apologize. "When things repeat themselves, camera is put to bed."

"You never know where that camera will find itself in bed."

She leads me out after John and Terry. Terry is asking John if his parents met in Haiti or Montreal.

"At a pot party," John says over his shoulder. "The next day, when he saw her, my dad says, 'Man…' Like man, you still dark, woman. Somebody forgot to turn on the lights."

"Was she angry?" Terry asks.

"Hell no, she only spoke French. He'd been with her all night and all morning and it still hadn't sunk in." Terry stops and watches John stride ahead of her. I follow them, moving down the inside of Elizita's caboose. "Was she that lovely?" Terry asks John about his mother.

"Or that good in bed?" John says over his shoulder. "Or was my old dad that damn stupid? I dunno, ma'am. That's the story as he tells it. Overawed by her, I'd say. He always was. And like Elizita says, if you don't find out about each other first night in bed, you spend the rest of your life in the dark, trying."

"Go on!"

His wit and intelligence surprises Terry, whose fingers land on him, to hit or push him as she does to me when she's amused by my banter. His bulk doesn't budge and her hand slides up his back.

"Hey, hey," he says over his shoulder.

"What's your real job?" Terry asks. "You're too bright to be a porter?"

"No, I got a worse job than the porter's, ma'am, I'm the accountant. Bookkeeper would be a better way to look at it. The guy who manages the money round here has got to be built like a linebacker and think like a quarterback."

He turns to look back at Elizita, leaning out the caboose window before we round the front and head across to our guest railcar.

"The bookkeeper," shouts Elizita, "is prepared to give you a float. A starter, like a complimentary silver dollar in a casino, to start you playing."

"Playing what?" I ask her to explain for the camera.

"Our slots," Elizita answers.

Through a door in one wall of the repair yard men in blue coveralls load aluminium containers onto a cart with huge rubber wheels that flop softly over everything, rails included. The top of the steel-walled refrigerator truck gleams through the high windows above the door in the corrugated wall. Beyond the gaping, roll-back exit doors at the other end, the railcars for a real train still rest at an actual station, but with no locomotive. The cart with the tractable pneumatic tires moves toward it and we watch it as we walk toward our sleeper (sleeping carriage, we would call them at home).

Elizita tugs my shoulder. "Let Terry have John to herself for a bit. He's an interesting man." She leads me to the other end of the sleeper that John and Terry have just climbed into with our luggage. She lets me climb the iron foot-ladder ahead of her, helping me up the steps with the camera by pressing her hands onto the back pockets of my jeans, then sliding them down the sides as if cleaning her hands off once I'm safely on the metal platform.

"You go in," she says, as she opens the door for me, then steps aside. "It's a half-car, but for you I'll call it a halfin', like whisky? You might need one soon."

I wonder if the whole car is as long as ones I've seen in old movies. I never counted the number of seats the marshal walked past, hunting for a bandit, who leapt from a horse and hid among the crowd on board. Cars were as long as the suspense of the search, I suppose.

Elizita hasn't turned on the light, and doesn't draw back the curtains. The place gives off a glazed darkness, extending from the wall of dark glass in the middle of the car. Put in to double the size with the reflection. No door or panel adjoins this half to the other half of the car. A wide carriage seat opposite the glass wall doubles as a bed-end.

"Why'm I made to play blind man's bluff?" I ask, but the phone rings.

"It's for you," she declares. "Set the camera down on the bed."

The back end of the cord-free receiver raps my knuckles.

Immediately I put the receiver to my ear, Terry asks, "What are you taking so long to do with El?"

She breathes out in that laboured way that signals she has prepared a minor tongue-lashing for me. "I see, I see," Terry exhales, but talking to an altogether different person, who must be John, showing her the accommodation, likely with the light on. She gets generously agitated when I don't reply right away.

"Well…I'm trying to take things in…"

"That's nice, very nice," says Terry, but again the tone tells me it's Terry to John, who's on the right side of her at this point, unlike myself. I sit down on the bed, trying to cope with Terry breathing at me on the phone, and Elizita, doing the same, now, in my ear.

"That's just lovely," I hear Terry say to John. Huffing, I think, because I haven't spoken, but her breath falters on the total exhale of exasperation. "Ooh, the trains. Ask Elizita if – when she was on the train to Bangor, looking at those pictures on the carriage wall of Newcastle, County Down with those cold beaches – ask her if she was always thinking of a hot place in Nevada, or – let me see – Polynesia?"

My eyes have adjusted enough to see El go pull a dress like a tunic, and an enormous belt from a closet. She holds it up and laughs at it. I see why it tickles her. The buckle's as big as the WWE champeen's belt.

"Daft, but goes well with this tunic?"

I nod.

"Our champion performers wear one. Men contenders, hulks and toughs, even weasels can't wait to take it off them."

"Go on, go on," says Terry, who for once has ignored the long pause at my end. "I'm waiting for El's answer, but dearie me. Mr. Pause moves on slow, very slow paws," she chides me like a child with a silly rhyme… "Ask her, I'll keep on the phone. And…does Elizita have an old high-backed railway carriage seat at the end of the bed, facing the wall?"

As always, Terry's detour from old carriage photos to carriage seats confuses me about what to ask first, but need I worry? "You know what I've realized," says Terry, "why a railcar, as they call it here in America…why it used to have just two doors for the whole car, and in Britain and Northern Ireland, each compartment had two doors of its own. Oh, ho, ho," she snorts and she pauses. "You don't know why?" She waits for me to supply an answer.

"I don't."

"El told me long ago. They designed every compartment with its own set of doors to make it more private, easier to have sex, if a couple found themselves on their own."

"Has drink been taken, more merry martinis, by any chance?" I try to turn irritation into a bit of humour.

"Guess."

"My guess is distance…" I get up and walk to the glass wall and turn to the carriage seat "…my guess is greater distances between the stops in America. People got in and out less often. More democratic, less stand-offish people in America. Americans didn't mind riding with everybody together in one big room, in the old days."

"That would be nice, riding together with everybody in one big room," Terry giggles.

"Are you still drinking?"

"Aren't you?" she answers. "What's wrong with that, 'specially if it's laid on, and I'm here waiting? Aren't I, John?"

I'm instantly annoyed, not at her bringing John into the phone call, but her using her prim and boozy "aren't." And I can hear the fabric of her clothes rasp as she rubs against some other scratchy material, the heavy upholstery of the carriage seat?

Breathing very emphatically she asks, "How it feels… do you remember?"

"What?"

"Sex in our own private compartment?"

"Vaguely," I say, and hold the phone away from my ear to catch the sound of silk coming from the direction of Elizita's closet. Low whistles of silk like a ghost train's as the folds of a light bathrobe encircle Elizita's body.

"Do you always do things in the half-dark?" I ask Elizita, and regret it right away for the way Terry will hear it.

El's side of the sleeping car is organized with Indian blankets: Mojave and Navajo, like the ones that prissy, mousy-mouthed Jennifer Jones wrapped about her in that movie, *Duel in the Sun*. She played a breed alongside Walter Huston, Joseph Cotton and Charles Bickford, and some-body incredibly tall – Gregory Peck. I remember holding Terry's hand while the prissiness smouldered on Jennifer Jones's mouth. I stared into the murk on her oiled and dark-ened face and into Terry's in the picture house. Jennifer Jones, a woman I always regarded as twitter-brained and simpering, sizzled like Elizita.

"Got to get the desert dirt off me," she announces.

Bead curtains, made from balls of lacquered goat dung drape the shower door. Elizita pushes her face through them and lets the gown slide down behind her.

It prompts me to send Terry's memories of sex in the dark adrift.

"Do you remember *Duel in the Sun*, Terry?"

No sound from the other end, and from the sound of it, the shower is short.

"A bit of a squeeze in there," says Elizita, stretching.

"Doubtless," says I, keeping my head down. I pick up and hold out the gown for her to put back on.

"I hate the shower's sliding door. Too like a goddamn guillotine. Fellas clutch their crotch if I wing it across."

"Less shock with the beads," I say in this luminous gloom, convinced she's using it like optical cosmetic, to keep the shape while glossing over the heavy weather on the private parts of her body she's bared.

Then I go "Oh, Jesus" at the ring of black mud she has perfectly stencilled round her eyes.

The truth at last. "For the crow's feet and wrinkly brow?" asks I, before I see the thick black frames on the Bette Davis, bad-ass-of-a-business-lass specials.

The truth – time for El to tell me, "No lenses." She takes them off and pokes her finger through. "They're to show I'm after serious brass fur serious trade."

With that she goes and turns a light on, to be seen, still holding her gown I handed her at arm's length, like it's the empty cabinet in a magic trick and her very visible body has just popped up beside it. Which makes my stomach take a leap in time, onto the back of Gruff Gordie's Triumph Bonneville, as he wove me on the pillion, in and out of the late Sunday traffic, along the white line, at 105 mph. Up the dual-lane stretch from Craigavad to Holywood.

Gordie's absurd tweed sports coat he always went out in scratched my hands as I clutched on to him, scratched like the hair shirt that never quite fit me.

"How does that effin' well feel? Effin' devastatin', right?"

That feeling flutters through my stomach, reaching into my backbone, which shakes like jelly when I get my mind off Gordie's bike and the phone rings.

I pick up and hear Terry chuckle without speaking, like she hasn't put the phone down.

"How does it feel, Gavin? Like a ride on a train back when?"

Then, off the top of my head or pit of my stomach I'm blurting out Gordie's hell-rider yell, "Like doing the ton and ready to detonate."

"The ton on a train, hon…?" Terry rhymes me into the ridiculous with the *hon* – Terry, the linguist and sometimes poet, who persecutes me with puns when she's playful.

I know what I mean by detonate, even if Terry doesn't. Elizita is turning my TV documentary into Technicolor TNT. I see it in her face. She waits, waits, looks at me and she knows I hear it in the swallows Terry takes at the other end of the line.

Next thing I know, El lets me feel her breath on the corner of my mouth as she puts her chin on my shoulder… "What do you spy with your little eye when I turn on the ceiling?"

Her breath retreats. "I heard what Elizita said," Terry tut-tuts. "So, who's doing a turn on the ceiling…?"

I still look up, though.

In the painted glass that covers the near end of the ceiling, young girls are washing themselves down with soap. Some are on their knees, looking up, rubbing at the legs and the genitals of the girls looming over them. They are laughing, lashing each other with soap.

Elizita comes round to sit beside me, alongside where I have fallen back to look up at Terry with a facecloth thrust between her legs. Her young face above me says what I hear from her mouth on the phone, which rings and El hands to me.

"God, what now?"

"Do you see?"

"See what?"

"See who? Sandy!"

I haven't noticed because of the girls and their spectacular sudsing: a three-quarter length door, a man's head and shoulders, the tops of a short-sleeved Fair Isle pullover. The man, faceless under his cloth cap, his missing features shining down, emptily, eerily.

Shuffling the back of my head up the bed to the pillows, as soon as I see my face, reflected in the mirror-glass, I feel Elizita's fingers on my lips, the tips of the fingers hot, the lacquered silver nails, just hard.

"Now, go down t'other end. Take a seat, and have a lie down there," she tells me.

"I'm teed off with t'other," I tell her.

"Go."

I go and sit on the seat facing the wall, which I'm sure gives Terry complete access to me, and me, none to her.

"Lie down, you silly bugger. Take the weight off your legs." Elizita pushes me and thieves the phone from my fist as I fall back.

At this end of the car's curved ceiling, a veranda looks out over a stretch of cracked red earth with one tree on it. A man lies on the bare veranda with no railing, a woman beside him. They both peer down over their naked hips, genitalia and feet pointed at another couple, sitting at the veranda end. They, in turn, look at another pair coupling, the woman's legs buckled tightly around the man's waist. The same girls I brushed by so long ago mate with men whose bodies have been worked underground or outdoors. The young men engaged with the girls have flattened stomachs and their hips are well honed. On the steps leading onto the veranda, a queue has formed of older men, whose stomachs sag into globes with no definition. They are obviously miners, in jeans and bare chested, their bodies made interesting by work, by various labours and forms of neglect, none contoured by youth anymore. Some have a black confetti of coal dust on their upper body or have been painted around head, neck and forearms with a labourer's tan.

"You want Gavin," Elizita says into the phone, then nods several times as if for extra assurance to whoever has a hold of the other end. "Okay, here he is, John."

"Gavin," John says to me, "your wife insists that she is putting her whole mind and body into getting you that half-crown for the Tonic. What is a half-crown? And is the "tonic" like, for gin and tonic, or code for drugs?"

"Half a crown is a coin, in today's money, about two dollars," I answer, calculating for inflation as best I can. There is a courteous gasp. "And the joint we shared, John, was the old Tonic Cinema in Bangor, where we courted in the dark, cuddled, out of the Northern Irish rain to watch *South Pacific* or big, spacey Westerns like *Duel in the Sun, The Searchers,* or *The Big Country*. But so's you know, our real distances were measured with fingers and lips. We were right next to the big thing we were groping for in the dark."

The railcar begins to bump and shunt as soon as Elizita jabs a switch. The expression on her face says the two aren't synchronized. But I don't believe her face, she must have signalled the coupling of the car to a locomotive or the rest of the train we saw down the tracks at the platform.

"Some scenery to get us going. I luv to save a Midnight Special for special people," she jabs me.

She turns a round dimmer switch and the view to the other half of the railcar comes on across the wall. I swing my feet and use my arms to push me up, foment this see-through wall.

Now, *that* woman sitting on the other side of the glass with a black man standing beside her – her lips going loose and louche on her. I remember making love to *her* on a Belfast-County-Down-Railway train, trying to lie on one of the long door-to-door seats in a carriage that held only the two of us, squeezed tight-in to each other, so as not to fall off onto the floor.

Taking turns, one on top of the other, flinging out a hand to the other seat to keep us together, I remember the feel of wet lips and faces, of swimming down this clanking, metal river that smelt of musk and smoke, cinders and the scent girls put on. Not like the thick perfume Elizita daubs on herself, here and there, like she smatters herself and us, here and there, with her Brummie accent.

I nod through the window wall at where Terry sits.

"Comfy seat?" I ask her.

"Good for sitting down on. Hauling off the clodhoppers, if it's pelting out."

"Smart answer, ten points for that," I congratulate her.

"But it never rains in Nevada." I see Elizita's frown at Terry. "You got the weather wrong, luv."

"I'd get a wiggin' from Ms. Mathers over wrong friggin' weather, right?"

"Too friggin' right." They both double over. "And seat's at wrong end. Way 'way frum door, where John cum in."

"Is that John collective or singular?" I ask, to break this girls'-school swearing in the lav carry-on.

The railcar heaves, not with their silly belly laughs, but as cars lurch into motion, their coupling complete. Still bent-over, bum-up, it bumps Elizita against me on the seat.

John I see sits, perched beside Terry, pretending to whistle. Elizita straightens up, purses her lips, pretending to answer his pretend call.

"Now, 'bout that client of yours, John. You forgot to check her bona fides. But you'll still bet salary on't she be clean, right?"

"That client of yours" rings out of Elizita's mouth, like an old-time cash register.

"Now, this client of mine… Will you vouch for his bona fides, Ter?" Elizita's arm is around me to ask. "If you do, is it a done deal?"

Terry takes hold of John's hand. "As we smart grammar school girls well know." She smirks at me through the glass, then round at John. "Like dotting the i's, like circling the number of the right answer on an intelligence test at school. We're sure to score 100%."

Articulate tart is Terry.

"All's left now is to spit on our hands and shake."

"Spit on whatever you like, I'll shake," says I.

"Cross El's heart," John tells me, "and hope to die."

An Ulster Glossary of Utterances

any road means the same as *any way*, as in high road and highway, used interchangeably.

Barter Book is a ledger in which any items up for barter are listed beside any items offered in exchange.

Brummie is the word derived from Birmingham to describe its inhabitants or used as an adjective to describe anything originating in Birmingham, the accent, for example.

cleat is a metal fastener with a male and female connection used instead of a button and button hole on a shirt, jacket or similar garment

diddies are synonymous with breasts in Ireland, and used to convey the plumpness and mobility of breasts. The word can also be used to emphasise the opposite, for example: "as small as a mouse's *diddy.*"

dirty git could have the spelling *gait* for *git* and both would be the Ulster word for goat with different pronunciations in different counties and within different parts of the county (North and South Down, for example) and in different parts of Belfast.

drumlin is a standard geographical term for a round, mound like hill of rich soil left behind by the glaciers in the ice age. Parts of North Down in Ireland are composed of drumlins, graphically described by geography teachers as "basket of eggs topography."

geek, meaning look, can be used as a verb or a noun, as in "take a geek." The look one takes when one geeks is not dainty like in "peek," but short, sharp, more insistent and intrusive.

gub refers to the face, particularly the lower part around the mouth. "Shut your gub!" tells you in no uncertain terms to shut your mouth.

do the ton is a term for reaching the speed of one hundred miles per hour.

guard's van is the compartment reserved for the guard and the goods carried on the train, usually coupled to the end of the train.

halfin' is a half glass of whisky.

lurgy is always dreaded and is a nameless virus that lays one low. Sometimes referred to as the flu, but more often something indefinably debilitating.

peeler – Sir Robert Peel founded the first police force in England, and as a consequence the first policemen were called peelers thereafter in dubious honour of the founder.

RAG week let students raise a ruckus and money for charity. On RAG Day, they dressed up and hit the streets with a parade and tin cans for collecting the money.

training-slip is a light women's swimsuit, worn by competitive swimmers in the fifties, when regular swimsuits were too often made of heavier fabric. The term, swimming costume, was still in use by the older generation in the fifties, and traces of that were still evident in regular swim suit designs.

wiggin' when used here means to grab by the hair and shake. In the old days it was the actual wig that was grabbed and pulled from the head to shame the wearer. In parliament or the courts, the action could be carried out to officially disgrace a person in high position. Nowadays, it is used metaphorically, if at all. Although in the fifties, a student could still find themselves grabbed by the hair and shaken for some grievous error in class.

ACKNOWLEDGEMENTS

"Arrivederci" first appeared in *Ambit*; "Sittings in a Green Room" in the *Fiddlehead*; a micro version of "The Dark Barber" was published in the *Antigonish Review*; "Tennis" in the *Carter V. Cooper Short Fiction Anthology Series,* Book Three, and *ELQ/Exile Quarterly* 37.1; "Sisters in Spades" in the *Carter V Cooper Short Fiction Anthology Series,* Book Four, and *ELQ/Exile Quarterly* 38.2; "El" (original version as "Quid Pro Quo") was a runner-up in the 1998 *Malahat Review* novella competition.